DOODLEBUGS & SPITFIRES

Memories and Short Stories

by Peter Carroll

COPPERHILL MEDIA

A Division of Copperhill Technologies Corporation

http://www.copperhillmedia.com

DOODLEBUGS & SPITFIRES
Memories and Short Stories
by Peter Carroll

Published by
Copperhill Media
A Division of Copperhill Technologies Corporation
158 Log Plain Road
Greenfield, MA 01301
USA

Cover Design by Copperhill Media
Background photo acquired through iStockPhoto.com
Vintage Photos – Contributor: kemie

ISBN-10: 0-938581-03-2
ISBN-13: 978-1-938581-03-8

http://www.copperhillmedia.com

Paradise Walk

The Goodrington Cliff Walk is a popular evenings stroll for visitors and local residents of the picturesque Torbay, Brixham Harbour, the neighbouring coast, and the magnificent Devonshire landscapes. Its famous lights have made it a regular attraction for the pleasure boats working in Torbay, and they regularly run evening trips from Paignton Harbour to witness the illuminated cliff walk from the seaward side.

And yes, there is a story behind the circumstance that the Goodrington Cliff Walk is known locally as Paradise Walk, and it begins with a young and gallant, but poor lad named Ivan who fell in love with a girl from a wealthy family.

In the spring of 1929, Ivan Jones, only eighteen years old, having arrived by a special train with many other young men of his age, was stunned by the sheer beauty of the golden sands of Goodrington in the southwestern coastal resort of Torbay.

He had quickly regained his self-esteem when, after a year without work and the coal mining industry having reached a decline, he was given the opportunity to help build the new Goodrington Cliff Walk as part of a Government incentive to find jobs for unemployed South Wales miners, nicknamed *Taffies*.

It meant leaving his mother and father for the first time, but it made a lot of sense, and it also gave him the opportunity to leave the nest and fend for himself.

He was in his prime, and this new opportunity gave him renewed impetus to make something of his bleak life after being stuck in the coal pits, like his dad and granddad before him, since he left school.

In those days, travel was expensive, and the working fraternity was rarely able to afford a car. And to telephone someone as far away as the Rhondda Valley was out of the question, especially when Ivan planned to send money home for his hard-up parents who were drastically on the breadline.

But letter writing, at least, kept him in touch, and, on opening his first letter mailed to home, his mother radiated a broad smile. Ivan wrote he was fairly happy and was comfortable in the digs right near the seashore. In fact, it was just opposite to the area where he had worked with a score of other taffies from the mines.

Their skill was indispensable in the building of the new cliff walk, and it meant a substantial wage, something he had missed for months gone by since the mine closed down.

After the dust, the pollution, and the darkness he endured working in the dark mines, and because he had known nothing else, Ivan discovered in the seascape of Torbay, which he called heaven, the smell of the Devon sea breeze, the magnificent scenery, and a sense that all was well with the world. At last, he could spread his wings just like he had always wanted.

Despite his young age, he had gained great experience, since he started in the mines at the age of fourteen. Onlookers watched with admiration from a safe area as the miners hacked away the dangerous overhangs and chiseled out the new pathways zigzagging upwards to the top of the cliff.

In the course of a year, the work was well on schedule. Nevertheless, the miners had a little hassle from local people who objected about despoiling the natural rock face, almost as if they were blaming them.

On one occasion, the abuse became so intense, work was suspended, and Ivan feared for his job, that they might do as the objectors wanted and abandon the project.

But some men, escorted by a policeman, came and broke up the party of about ten and all was well again. Ivan took the advice offered by the police, just to ignore them if they started again, and not to get involved.

The workers were more than happy to do just that, fearing their job maybe on the line if they hit back at the abuse thrown at them.

But it all seemed to quieten down, and the miners were left to continue their specialized work in peace.

Later, two prominent archaeologists, interested in the type of rock found there, visited the site. The rocks and stones were deposited when the whole area, including Paignton, lay in a broad depression surrounded by mountainous ridges, creating the jumbled and fruitcake-looking rock known as Breccia. In those arid conditions, irons within the rocks were oxidized, turning them red, very different from the sedimentary black coal rock to which Ivan was accustomed.

But all was not smooth going. The rock face was somewhat deceptive, and the reaction to an over-enthusiastic twosome took a turn for the worse when a gigantic span of rock came away with a sudden surge taking the miners with it and into the sea below. Ivan, a keen swimmer, attempted to rescue them, but the outgoing tide washed the fallen miners out to sea, and they were lost forever.

The gallant Ivan broke a wrist in the effort, which prevented him from working for a couple of weeks, but the local paper made such a story out of his brave gallantry that his employers were deemed to allow him sick pay in the like, and that they may receive unfavourable publicity if they declined.

At that time, as providence had it, Ivan met a local girl, a nurse in the hospital where he had his wrist plastered. It was one of those magic moments when boy meets girl, and they were instantly attracted to one another, like it truly was love at first sight.

He learned that Andrea was studying at the University College of the South West of England, and, as part of her practical training, was assigned for a few weeks to nearby Paignton Cottage hospital. In those days, her family would have been well off to afford her place there, so Ivan was well aware that she must have come from a well to do family, in a different class from him. With this in mind, when Andrea invited him home to meet her parents, he was particularly apprehensive, but Andrea told him, it was no problem, that her parents respected her feelings and trusted her.

Regretfully, Andrea was to learn that they were not quite so delighted about her choice in Ivan, stating that there was all the time in the world to think about romance, and she should concentrate on her studies. And, anyway, they expected she would find someone in her own class and not a common or garden miner who could offer her nothing but grief.

"Ivan, I am afraid I am obliged not to go out with you anymore. I am dreadfully sorry, but it is my parents, you see. They only want the best for me."

Ivan angrily responded in no uncertain terms. What in heaven's name did 'obliged' mean? Did she not love him as she said she did?

Andrea, in tears, explained that her parents would decline to pay for her University education if she continued to see him, that the natural thing was for him to wait for her, and when she qualified, they could see each other again.

"And how long would that be?"

"I have completed two years, so that makes another three. I am aiming for a doctorate, you see."

"Three years is a long time, Andrea. Can we hold out for that long? And what's to say when you are fully qualified, you won't have gone off of me by then?"

"It will be a test of our love for each other, Ivan. Surely, we shall keep in touch, of course. And we can write letters to each other like you do with your parents."

"But even then, if your parents are against me, what then?"

"I shall be independent by then, of course. It would be a shame if my parents didn't accept you then. But let time take its course. I am sure they will, when, after three years, they will see that we still love each other. How could they reject you then?"

Realising how important Andréa's studies were to her helped him to agree to that arrangement. It also made him realise just how valuable a sound education is, persuading that he too had the enthusiasm and the sheer dogged ambition to make something of himself.

Ivan became so enthused, knowing how much they were in love, that he decided to take on something he would never have done before with the notion that he was not intelligent enough. But in spending time with Angela, he realised they were on an even keel. He took up an opportunity to partake in a course in geology offered by the government, another special scheme offered to certain groups of unemployed who showed scope and enthusiasm.

He thought of how it would have been if it hadn't been for his move to Devon, courtesy of the government scheme, that he would be stuck in Wales, hopelessly seeking work. But now, given the opportunity to better himself and that coupled with the hope for a future with Andrea, he knew things were about to change. It was that, which helped him to face the absence with his new found love in Andrea.

Andrea continued her studies at the University College, and her search for detail proved to be a real passion between them, both given their correspondence exchange once a week. He would telephone her and she him, but that was limited because of the expenditure in those days.

And taking on his new venture, Ivan's studies led him to learning all about the area in which he worked. He discovered, there had once been a convent near the beach at Goodrington, also that it had been temporarily converted into a hospital when a shipload of sick sailors from abroad were tended there.

He also learned that Goodrington was known as Godrintona in the Domesday Book and was situated in the 'tun,' a hamlet or farm, of Godhere, later called Goderiington. It was owned by Robert Morcelles Kent in the time of Henry III and chronicled as Gorrenton Sands in 1617.

Also, a leftover from the Viking invasion of Britain, a gold Viking arm ring was found there. And on 14 August 1484, King Richard III granted his esquire Thomas Tunstall the manor or lordship of 'Goodrington next Totnes in Devon.'

Maintaining their contact and occasionally meeting in secret when Angela was breaking from University, it was as though the couple was made for each other, each with their broad regional dialects. They often teased each other imitating the other's dialect and discovered just how important a rich sense of humour could sustain a deep, loving relationship.

Ivan wrote home, telling his parents about Andrea, and he looked forward to the time when the pressure of work allowed him a break enough to proudly show her off, when the time came and they were together for good, her father having graciously presented Andrea with one of the new-fangled motor cars for her eighteenth birthday, making it easier to travel and visit his parents.

It came to pass that Ivan was rewarded for all the hard work he had put into the new Rock Walk. He passed with honours all his studies and was presented with a diploma and a promotion to project manager, the youngest ever to accomplish that position with the mining firm.

Andrea's family did realise and accept that Ivan would, no doubt, become their new son-in-law. In fact, they admired him for the work he had done and, indeed, the work he was presently doing, which was not without its obvious dangers.

"You get accustomed to the feel of the rock," Ivan explained. "It seems to talk to you if under stress, making a certain creaking noise, and you know when to stand back."

"I expect, it is the sort of job you can get a real feeling of achievement," supposed Andrea's father. "It's hard, and you have obviously got to be tough to do it, but I guess the end product is what it is all about."

"And the owner of Paignton Zoo had said he will supply the plants and bushes when we are finished," continued Ivan, "in order to cover up the scars. You can't help them - it has to be - but Mr. Whitley has the right idea, and it will really set off the new cliff walk. I look forward to that."

"And I look forward to being among the first to take the cliff walk arm in arm with you, Ivan," said Andrea. "They say lights will be set up to illuminate the area at night. How romantic will that be?"

The three years had quickly passed, and they were together for real.

"Yes, Andrea. It will be. It is all going to be quality stuff. No messing with us Taffies, you know."

How perfect it all was, and how truly fortunate Ivan felt he was, with a new life, and soon, hopefully and deservedly so, a new wife, after feeling confident enough to ask Andrea to marry him when the occasion was right.

Given the horrible depression of the time, a new light seemed to shine on Ivan, like the new attraction that was to be Goodrington, when too the hordes of holiday visitors came by train to the new Goodrington Sands station built in 1928.

A boating lake and children's playground was in place, and, given the beautiful stretch of gentle golden sands with plenty of rocks to explore, there was something for everyone. When, in 1931, the cliff walk was completed, it was as if Ivan, with his colleagues, had made their own distinct mark on Mother Earth.

When one evening our couple took the walk from Paignton along Roundham Head, descending the stairways and gentle downward slopes, they stopped and looked out across the water seeing Berry Head Lighthouse flickering in the distance.

Ivan proposed, and, of course, Andrea accepted. Perched high on the walkway, surrounded by Herbert Whitley's new plants, flowers and shrubs, the coloured illuminations sparkling the beginning of a brand new era.

It was soon known as *Paradise Walk* for obvious reasons, and the red Devon cliffs lit up at night, presenting a warm welcome and giving Goodrington an ambience all its own.

Captain Letts' War

The Scapa Flow was often a dangerous place to be during the Second World War when German submarines were keen to cut supplies to the British mainland.

Britain was in the midst of a war, completely unprepared for what was happening, and on the face of it, looking like an unlikely force to defend against the mighty Hitler regime.

The brave men of the merchant navy not only had the might of the enemy submarine fleet to contend with but also the Stuka, too, the classic Blitzkrieg dive bomber of World War II, which was responsible for the bombing of Warsaw in Poland, culminating in the British declaration of war with Nazi Germany in 1939.

Nevertheless, brave men risked their lives to the fore with hope and faith in their hearts that they would get through without being spotted, their armless craft hopefully not been seen. But the enemy was resolute to starve the British into surrender, and for a while they were doing a pretty good job of doing just that.

Winston Churchill was frantically pushing the ministry of defense to speed up production of the weapons and materials of war and the training of new recruits in all the services.

It was the start for many women to do the work the men did before they were called up to fight the good fight; the husband would never again be the sole breadwinner.

But given old doubts women proved, given the necessity of the time, they could do just as well as their male counterparts.

But at the end of the day the country depended just as much on the merchant navy to feed and nourish the nation, to ensure Britain would not fall like Poland and France.

The resolute SS Crow had taken the risk despite the odds; she was on a special mission to deliver her cargo of scarce provisions come what may. But now she was hit.

The stern was holed, the enemy torpedo had found its mark. The Crow, a merchant ship, turned and faltered. Two of the ship's company instantly lost their lives as the huge explosion lifted their bodies, depositing them with debris into the calm sea.

7

Completely caught off guard, the remaining crew of seven, including the captain, was in absolute chaos.

The vessel, hit to the stern, was already beginning to roll over, and a plume of black smoke rose from the funnel.

Captain Letts knew the risk, his company, too. They had tossed a coin. Should they take the safe long way, which would add a day to their journey, or the short alternative, through enemy infested waters? They had been away from home too long. Wives, sweethearts, sons, and daughters anxiously awaited their return in time for Christmas.

The short route, failing any attack, would almost ensure they were with their beloved kin for Christmas. Letts pictured his wife, Ann, and Jeff, his son, and grandchildren Jason and Elizabeth who had lost their mother in a fatal road accident just a year before.

When the coin stopped spinning, it was heads for the short passage.

But the enemy had surfaced unseen to the stern. A beam of light came from the deck; the Crow was like a sitting duck waiting to be slaughtered. The captain could do nothing; they were at the mercy of the enemy. One of the men kneeled and prayed they may be spared, but rousing cheers could be clearly heard from the submarine's deck which meant a reward for them, their order were not to spare any foreign vessel, no matter what.

The time was up for the Crow, and the crew shivered in the brisk cold wind, waiting for the enemy's pleasure. There was nowhere to hide, nowhere to go given the suddenness of it all.

Another 'fish' came streaming through the steady drifting current to penetrate the twisting Crow amidships. This was the end. Letts knew it. A reel of black smoke spiraled into the night sky as the engine room exploded with huge force. He immediately ordered the survivors, four in all, to abandon ship, throw over the escape net and scramble for their lives to the lifeboats.

"Get the hell out of here, and row the boats out of sight!" was Letts' last command on board of the quickly sinking Crow.

Captain's mate John Ricard yelled to his captain to join them snappy, but he seemed not to respond, like he was in a state of shock, not believing what was happening, maybe not wanting to believe.

One seaman panicked and jumped headlong into the icy waters. The three others made it, ice cold and scrambling into the lifeboats and away.

Captain Letts hung on until the last, aiming to swim for it, clambering over the deck attempting to reach the nets alongside.

Without remorse, the enemy released a third fish as the flaming Crow, half sunk, twisted and turned. Letts made a final grab and hung on to the nets for his dear life. There was no place to hide; he stood out in the strong shaft of light beaming from the submarine like a sore thumb. He would have to make a jump for it and make for one of the lifeboats.

The third fish missed the Crow by inches but the tail rudder caught the nets, taking Letts with them, tangled in the strands. Now Letts knew he would die. His whole being was fading, yet he felt no pain. He would hang on till the last; he was that sort of guy.

But then something caught his eye, making him aware that the game was not over yet. The fish skimmed steadily through the waves into the darkness beyond the point where the survivors could see, and they thought their captain was a goner, that was for sure, swearing at the enemy who were now taking the dive, their mission accomplished.

But not quite. Well, not as far as Letts was concerned.

Somehow he managed to use the tangled nets as reins, pulling hard to the right to turn the fish, cutting and turning through the calm sea ahead and then, straightening out, heading back from whence it came. He was with the prevailing current now, so it was easier to hold steady as he used all the strength he could muster of his solid body to guide the fish through.

If he was to die, he was determined the sub would, too. He just about made out the hulk in the shadows as he saw the sub in full dive red alert, and he prayed he would make it before the torpedo drained its fuel and the sub had submerged.

Letts men saw him again as the bright moon highlighted his progress, realizing what their Captain was about. But with mixed emotions, on the one hand, wanting him to destroy the enemy, and on the other, hoping he would miss, but knowing that if he did, his chances of survival were minimal.

They applauded their brave captain, holding their breath and hanging on for him, just in case there was a miracle.

An ominous thud and then a frightening scraping sound made way for a huge explosion which followed, illuminating the night sky, like a beacon with a cascade of white, red, and crimson jets of flame.

Captain David Letts had won his war, but, seemingly and sadly, not his life as the remaining crew, glad to be alive, would tell the story of their brave captain.

***

Letts' son, Jeff couldn't hide his emotions when he explained to his two kids that their Grandfather would not be spending Christmas with them this year. "But Nanny will be here, so you must be very good," he said.

"Then who's doing Father Christmas this year?" enquired ten-year-old Jason with a mischievous grin.

Jeff raised a brave smile remembering how Jason had pulled off Father Christmas' beard the year before and discovered it was his granddad. How, too, his six year old daughter Elizabeth reacted when Jason told her of his discovery.

"There's no such person as Father Christmas," she replied. "We all know he is Grandfather Christmas!"

"I expect, I shall have to do the honours then, Jason," Jeff exclaimed. "Do you mind if I am Father Christmas, though, will that be okay?"

Jason whispered into his dad's ear: "Until Elizabeth is old enough not to believe in him anymore. But I will always believe in Grandfather Christmas."

***

Yet on a Scottish beach David Letts thought of his past; memories drenched his mind in never ending flash backs, as if reaching out to everything that had happened during his lifetime. Was this death or life? Had he managed to untangle himself from the net holding him to a torpedo's tail fin?

Recollections emerged as he felt his soul floating, suspended in space, as if like waiting for judgment. Then how would they deal with his case?

He distinctly heard the voice: "David Letts, you may return. Your past is incomplete, and you have so much more to learn and do, because you are a spirit of true grit. You are among the elite!"

The flashing stopped, and he was alive, stranded on that lonely beach, his body numb but strangely no more pain. But the world was again within his reach.

One man and his dog found David and soon he was in a hospital, miraculously reaching full recovery.

His mission in life was yet to unfold and eventually another story will be told.

Letts eventually died at the age of 84. Grandson Jason compiled two poems in remembrance of his courageous grandfather.

Captain Letts' War (Poem)

SS. Crow's stern was holed
The torpedo found its mark
The crew ice cold
Scrambling in the dark

Captain Letts knew the risk
His men too
They'd thrown the disc
Came up tails: plan red two

The danger, red two: enemy infested waters
But it would cut the time in half
To see wives, sons and daughters
Alas, a surfaced submarine lit up their path

No remorse, the enemy were in for the kill
Another torpedo penetrated the bow
Letts and his men knew the drill
It was the end of Crow they knew it now

Scrambling down the escape nets
The lifeboats lowered port side
Crew first, followed by Captain Letts
But there was nowhere to hide

The game wasn't over yet
The sinking Crow faltered, Letts held tight
Hanging on ready to jump, ready set...
Yelled to his men: row boats out of sight

A third torpedo missed the gutted Crow
But caught the net entangled in its tail
Taking Letts with it into the Scapa Flow
He struggled to free himself to no avail

Letts knew he would die
His whole being was fading, he felt no pain
But then something caught his eye
The twisting turning: he was back again

He saw the sub in full dive red alert
He was almost on collision course but not quite
He tugged the net and saw the nose divert
Letts had not given up the fight

Now on true course he'd finish the bastards
The explosion lit up the sky
The Crow was still visible: its mast-heads
Captain Letts had gone out on a high.

Captain Letts Lives (Poem)

Letts thought of his past
Memories flashing in the mind
Some had become overcast
Others left behind

How quick the flashes are
Recollections constantly emerge
Vital Experiences from afar
Then the final surge

The time to face the music now
Letts soul was floating in space
Waiting for judgment: when, how?
How would they deal with his case?

David Letts you may return
Your past is incomplete
So much more to learn
You are among the elite

The flashing stopped. He felt real again
Stranded on a lonely beach
His body numb, no more pain
The world within his reach

His mission in life was to unfold
Another story to be told...

The Guy in the Train

We were relaxing in the garden when it started. "A-Tis-shoo!"

Vanessa sneezed violently and said it was probably hay fever.

"Bless you."

"Thanks, Phil" she smiled with those gorgeous eyes.

We both worked in the computer-programming department of a large firm in London. I took a shine to her as soon as I saw her. That wonderful slim and attractive figure did everything for her (and for me) and she was intelligent, too! I have never seen a woman look so good in a standard female business stripe suit.

But being a very large and busy commercial office, I rarely had the opportunity to try and start some sort of intelligible conversation with her at work.

But one day after work and making for home on Paddington station, I saw her on the platform and deliberately boarded the same carriage as she. Fortunately, it turned out, we regularly commuted on the same route and became friends; most of our travelling time was taken up in conversation and made the boring task of travelling much quicker and nicer. We sort of clicked somehow from the start.

We lived in the same town thirty miles up line from the London office. When our friendship developed, I wanted more. I just couldn't stop thinking about her; I was besotted by her - everything I had ever looked for in a woman was there. I really wanted badly to date her, but the jump from just friends to anything more - I wasn't sure. You know, the usual thing, would it spoil a rich friendship and all that! I went for it, took the risk, I was that keen - there was only one way to find out ...

Well, I had already done my research – very prudently, I might add – like did she have a current relationship, and so on and so forth. Turned out, she had been in a relationship, but not heavy and, for reasons undisclosed, they did not gel.

I was thinking go for it, mate – you have clicked at the right time. This girl is a peach and would surely be taken off the available list in a very short time. She had said of a couple of guys I knew at work, how they kept badgering her for a date and how she got to loathe their persistence, then going on to say they stood no chance because they were everything she hated in a guy, very macho and making out they were a magnificent example of manhood.

Me? Well, I was taking it all in, got to know the names of the guys involved, so I could avoid behaving like they were towards this very attractive girl I was oozing to wine and dine and that just for starters. The dessert, I was hoping, would follow with coffee at my place.

One evening after work, I took the plunge. I asked if she would share a meal with me. It was a lovely warm summer evening, so I suggested we buy a Chinese and gorge ourselves in my garden. She was a free agent, and so was I. So why not go for it? That is what I told her.

I think, I saw her eyes glint, those very appealing blue eyes, highlighted by strands of blonde hair shimmering in the breeze as we left the 5:45 Clipper from Paddington and made for the station car park. She was really something.

And she took her time to answer. There was me, thinking I had blundered. I was ardently looking for her body language but could not make out if it was for or against.

Imagine my sigh of utter relief when she teased that she would try anything once, so we collected our cars, made for the Chinese takeaway and headed for my place.

We had just completed our meal with a glass of wine, and my mind was afire with amorous thoughts. But I remembered how I had messed it with a former prospective girlfriend when I pushed the physical bit, but taking some advice from my happily married pal Frank, a work colleague, I played the cool guy and played on the emotional stance, which, I admit, is really my scene anyway. I showed her around my well-sized garden, which I had strived to keep nice, but it needed some more attention and soon. But for now I had other things on my mind, and that could wait, overgrown shrubs, weeds taboo! There were things in my life more important.

Although I had reason to believe otherwise when Vanessa showed such an interest in my rare blue rose, named Blue Moon.

"I love roses, and this is magnificent, the nearest rose to blue I have ever seen. I love to ponder in the garden. My mum always says you are next to God's heart in the garden. I am impressed, I really am. I love the way you have set everything out; it shows talent and caring. I have a cousin who believes one should talk to plants to get the very best out of them."

"True," I replied.

She smiled beautifully, and I felt closer to her than ever before.

At last, the first part of my plan had come true, to ask Vanessa for a date, well sort of, and all my concentration focused on her.

But you know what they say about best-laid plans. Things changed for the worst. Vanessa sneezed again but this time she grimaced with pain. She held her head down, hands clutching her tummy.

"That's not hay fever, Vanessa it's ... it's that guy on the train!"

She looked up at me looking baffled. "What on earth do you mean, Phil?"

"That baccy tin, Vanessa. The one you found the dope in. You sniffed it, didn't you?"

"You are making something out of nothing, Phil," she scowled.

Nevertheless, I was concerned, and despite Vanessa's disapproval I used my mobile to phone the Doc.

"It was no accident when he tripped like that, Vanessa - it was too pat - he was a real pain, he never took his eyes off you, the rat!"

"Look, Phil, he was a real nice guy. And please don't try to possess me. Anyway, we're not sure if the tin belonged to him, and we don't know if it contained drugs as such. We found it after he got off the train. Remember? It was the station stop before ours."

"It was his, alright, Vanessa. It fell from his pocket when he tripped, and you went to his assistance. It was all an act to attract attention. Don't you see that? I saw the way he was eyeballing you beforehand and the way he held your waist as you helped him to his feet. It's the guy on the train - whatever's in that tin is the root of your problem."

"See what the doc says, Mr. Green eyes - okay?" Vanessa responded. " So - whatever that was inside the tin, it reeked to high heaven, and, anyway, there was no sign of any drug element, simply some tiny pieces of balsa wood looking and smelling as though they'd been coated with something. That's all. We mustn't get paranoid about it, must we? I do believe, you are jealous.

"Look, Phil, you have absolutely no hold on me just because I agreed to share a meal with you. Right? Did you actually see the tin fall from his pocket?"

I hesitated to find an honest reply.

"There!" she grinned with a knowing look on her face, reminding me of my mother who always knew best.

She had put me in my place. I must have been insane talking like that, when all she needed was a little show of concern, and me being so possessive, too, I could make a right mess of all the things I had dreamed of. That bloody guy in the train!

I was just at the point of apologising when she slumped in the garden chair, knees crumpled, sliding on the plastic seat and legs spreading.

Now was the time to show her I did care. I lifted her from the chair and kicking open the French doors, then hurriedly took her through into the lounge, out of the heat of the sun, placed her on the settee and moved to pick up a wet flannel from the bathroom, folding it across her forehead, hoping that would revive her.

Soon the doctor arrived, and I was relieved that, despite Vanessa's objection, I had called him, and I sighed with relief when he said that Vanessa was okay. I showed him the Baccy tin with the contents inside and explained what had happened - that guy on the train.

"Just keep her cool for a while," he advised. "Allergies come and go. Maybe the smell of the dope started it off. It wasn't hay fever, mainly the heat. It has been a hot summer. Something in the air. Who knows? Or maybe just perhaps the time of the month. Look, she's smiling now!"

I turned to Vanessa. She was and her whole face glowed. What a relief! I was so worried.

"Thanks, Doctor," Vanessa said as she quickly revived. "I'm sorry, we have brought you out. I feel a bit of a fraud now," she confessed.

"You did the right thing. Here's a prescription, something to help you if you have another attack," the doctor handed her the form.

"So this dope you mentioned; will it have any lasting effect on Vanessa?" I asked as I showed the doctor out.

"Not at all. If one is working with it constantly, then the usual precautions should be applied. As a student, I remember using the dope in University for scientific experiments. I recognised the pungent smell. The pieces of balsa were probability off-cuts on something the guy you mentioned was working on."

It is generally referred to as aeroplane dope. In fact, it is still widely used, because it works. It is available and is fire proof. Like anything, dope has its drawbacks.

First and foremost, it smells really bad. Whenever you hear the word, "dope" or any derivative of it in reference to drugs ("doped up", "dopey", etc.) it comes from this type of paint. The solvents in it will affect you and kill lots of brain cells if you don't use adequate protection for your respiratory system. That means charcoal mask at minimum.

Additionally, dope has a high rate of shrinkage

"But take it from me," the doctor continued, "in this case it was virtually harmless; to wash after contact is the rule of thumb."

I saw the Doctor off, thanking him for his call and his advice.

Vanessa felt lots better.

"I think, I love you," she said as it started to rain. "I guess I have done all along. I have never known anyone to be jealous over me before. You were acting almost as if we were married or something, the way you contacted the Doctor and everything!"

We kissed. Up to then it had just been friendly pecks on the cheek. This was our first real kiss. I had waited so long for this moment. Wonderful, fantastic! We deserved each other.

"Glad you told me that, darling," I stuttered excitedly feeling my heart beating madly, "be... because I was just about to tell you the same. I love you very much."

"And, anyway, you need somebody to keep you off the dope sniffing," I laughed.

"And you need someone to mow the lawn and tend the roses. I noticed the sad condition of your roses. Look, go take a look at them, covered in black spot, black fly and I don't know what! They need a woman's touch."

"I'd rather just look at you right now. Your beauty shames any rose. And talking of a woman's touch, come here and let me feel your kiss once more. You ought to know, it has been said I'm greedy when it comes to home comforts."

"You smooth talker, you" Vanessa smiled.

Now we both regularly share the garden and the house, not to mention the bed.

And the car. And we got married, too!

It was fate, thanks to the guy on the train.

Brave New World

Come Armistice Day on November 11th, I will be buying a poppy to commemorate another remembrance day, remembering all those souls of all nations who have died as a result of war.

Then, taking in the numerous wreaths surrounding the cenotaph in my hometown, the mind invariably flashes back. The march of time has taken its toll, joints stiffen and ache, not so flexible as when we danced and celebrated in the streets at the end of World War II. The hair thins and recedes, but we were fortunate indeed to survive the onslaughts of that terrible war when thousands upon thousands perished. We were given the opportunity to grow old in a brave new world, fit for the returning heroes. A world we could rebuild from the rubble, to start anew. Everything was going for us. It was going to be a great new future. We had every reason to rejoice. It was victory in Europe that day, May 9, 1945. I was just eleven.

The lights were switched on again, the restrictions of war almost gone. The blackouts were torn down, air raid shelters demolished, gas masks disposed of.

For those of us who grew up during the war, it was a little confusing. We had known no different. That's how it was, the bombs dropping down, the dash to the shelters, the dogfights above, Spitfires, Hurricanes and Messerschmitts. Every day was an adventure.

I can remember it as if it were yesterday. Every time those wreaths appear, I am transported back in time asking my mum: "When will Dad be home?" He had been gone a whole year, but it seemed like a lifetime. He was in the Royal Air Force fighter command serving as a pilot, and I was terribly proud of him, boasting to my pals that he was an ace pilot and, when we saw a Spitfire zooming overhead, it was always my dad flying it. Then we would mimic the aeroplanes, arms fully outstretched and running and twisting between each other, and there always had to be the good and the bad guys and invariably resulted in more German aircraft being shot down than ours, but in my heart I was hoping it would never be my dad. I tried to convince myself, he was a cut above the rest, and he was always the one doing the chasing, never the other way around. Well, he was my dad, wasn't he - and 'one of ours'!

My mum didn't reply immediately to my question. She looked remorseful and sad, but I could tell, she was having difficulty to put on a brave smile.

"Jack, you will have to be very brave. You see, your father has been reported missing after being shot down in France."

I was flabbergasted: "No, that can't be Dad! He would never get shot down. He is the best pilot in the world! I know it! They must have made a mistake." But, nevertheless, I felt the tears running down my cheeks as mum held my head against her breast.

"We must hope, Jack - that's all. Let us believe that he is safe. Perhaps, someone on our side in France has taken him in, maybe hiding him, or even if he is a prisoner of war, at least he will be still alive and maybe we shall hear soon. So let's keep our chins up and hope and pray."

Mum was an angel. I felt that my concerns were hers shared and, looking back, I was so glad she came out with the truth and told me what was happening, that there was a good chance that dad may have been killed, but we vowed not to ever think that way.

"I shall say a special prayer to God every night, Mum" I vowed.

"And so shall I, Jack. Tell you what, let's say one together." And even now I can remember those words giving me hope along with mum's warm smile.

After that, my pals asked why we never played the spitfire games, but somehow I just wanted to forget, persuading them to play other games instead. I never said why. I could not bring myself to tell them that, maybe, my dad had been shot down, but the trouble was they would invariably ask about him, saying that they wished they were old enough to be a pilot.

But all the while, us youngsters were being reminded almost every night that there were so many more bombers up there that had not been shot down and huddled in the family Anderson shelter at the bottom of the garden, along with my elder brother, mum, and my pet marmalade cat, Tibs.

The drone of the engines seemed to vibrate the corrugated sides of the shelter, even though they were covered in soil. My elder brother Alan took over the role of the head of the family, my dad being in the war, and I objected to him bossing me about like he was my dad, but looking back, he was only caring with the best intentions, and some nights we were joined by his pal Jack, one of his Air Training Cadets. He was a great guy who taught me how to play card games to keep our minds off of what was going on in the skies above us, but we always knew from the dull throbbing sounds of the engines, that those German planes were full of bombs, which could fall on us at any minute, hearing the occasional screech when they were released, pausing the card game, looking at each other intently until we heard the resulting horrific explosion, knowing that we were safe. But one night two, three, maybe more bombs exploded very near, and the whole earth shook and rumbled as I closed in to mum and squeezed her hand. The loud rumble seemed to be never ending, and I closed my eyes hoping it would soon stop and praying that perhaps my dad was flying again and chasing those nasty planes away.

When at last the noise died down and I raised my head, I saw Alan peering through the sackcloth curtain at the entrance of the shelter, yelling that it looked as though the bombs had made a direct hit on a house just down the road, that there were flames and smoke everywhere, that he would go out and see if he could help. Mum didn't like that idea at all but he insisted, saying it was probably someone we knew, and they may be needing some crucial help.

But then I realised something. Tibs was missing. He had possibly scampered with the resounding noise of the bombing. Then I felt terribly guilty, that I should have been watching him more carefully. But he was gone. Where? I just had to go out and find him.

"Wait until the all clear siren has gone," mum advised, holding me back, "and then you must be careful because there will probably be dangerous shrapnel and debris everywhere. I have a feeling our windows have been smashed in with the blast"

I looked at her pleading to let me go take a look, but she resisted saying that cats are cleverer than we may think, that Tibs would return of his own accord. "You'll see if I'm not right!" she assured.

But all the same, I was on tenterhooks. I found so much comfort in Tibs to offset the possibility that dad may never return, the sound of his rich deep purr as I stroked him, the way he rubbed his wet nose against mine. He was a cat to be treasured.

But things did not look good with Dad missing in action, Tibs still missing after two days and learning that one of my school colleagues, Doreen Williams, had been killed along with her family in the direct hit of a house just five numbers away. All this was very traumatic and all at once, the war did not seem so much of an adventure for me anymore or any of my pals in the street.

But there were always those grown-ups who cheered us, the 'good Samaritans' that helped keep everyone going. Especially the elderly, they were always there to help and dish out positive thoughts that soon the war would be over, and we could live a normal life again.

There was the 'community' shelter we could go to if we were out and about when the air raid siren sounded, and you can bet your life there was always the 'comedian' to arouse laughter and delight and the singers who spurred us on with the joy of the sing-song that became a must during those times, mimicking all the wartime artists like Vera Lynn, Gracie Fields and George Formby, to name just a few who were, like Winston Churchill, a positive element to raise those subdued spirits.

Somehow we youngsters never got bored; there was always something to do when food was rationed and a few pennies to be made collecting acorns for the pig farms. We were quite poor and, with dad being away, lived on a limited income. I wonder now, how ever did my mum manage with food rationing feeding our hungry mouths? But she did. I remember her bountiful suet puddings served with a dollop of treacle, bread and dripping or condensed milk, packets of dried eggs sent over to ease our food shortage and shipped in from the USA, lashings of winkles and sprats to give us the protein we needed.

We bathed just once a week come Friday. The bath was situated beneath a large fold-down table in the kitchen, and mum filled it with hot water from the gas copper, which was also used for the Monday washing and boiling, and topped up with each bathing, I was usually the last when a tidemark appeared around the edge.

I helped mum with the cleaning and polishing, and one of my regular chores was to clean the eating utensils. I also made handkerchiefs from old sheets, toilet paper or from newspaper. Mum taught us how to fend for ourselves and looking back, she was a great mum, like so many bringing their children up during those war torn days. I remember doing the mangling for her after school on washdays after she had hand washed the clothes and such,

I still cherish that special time we were raised, and somehow we managed to keep happy despite the consequences of what might and could happen each night the bombers came,

The days went by, and I had to live with the notion that Tibs may not return but never dared think that about Dad. If I ever mentioned him maybe not coming back, mum would simply place her fingers on her lips and beckon me to hush with that certain encouraging smile.

Soon came preparations for D-Day, and troops could be seen everywhere awaiting orders. US, Canadians, Indian and most servicemen from the commonwealth were in abundance, and somehow I felt that soon everything would be alright, that we would catch that nasty man called Hitler and Dad would come home.

"Boys, I have received a telegram," my mum told me not too long after all the troops had left, transported by air and lorry out from Northolt and other nearby bases and airfields. I remember literally hundreds of Dakota Aircraft pulling gliders full of troops and the essentials of war.

Mums face beamed, she was over the moon, and I instantly knew what she was going to tell my brother and me. "Your dad is safe, and he will be home in days. Hooray!"

And would you believe, that very same day Tibs appeared poking his head through the cat flap.

That was one of the happiest days of my life.

It was a good omen and soon we were told, the war had been won. I was two months off my twelfth birthday.

The grown-ups went absolutely crazy, dancing and milling around. We had never experienced such joy, everybody was so happy, decorations were draped across the streets, and Union Jacks were everywhere. This was a new adventure and experience to behold.

In our road two long tables were set side by side. I shall never forget that very special day. Even though strict food rationing was still in force, the grown-ups somehow managed to fill the tables with an ample supply of food; spam, corned beef and sprat sandwiches and even a couple of home cultured chickens which was a real treat after the paste, dripping and condensed milk sandwiches to which we had become accustomed.

Then there was the 'afters' - blancmange, jelly and all sorts of homemade cakes. It is difficult now to understand what this meant to us at the time. It was the first time for years that our stomachs were really full.

Of course, we all dreamt it would be the perfect world from then on. Hitler's reign of terror was finally crushed for all time, and we at home were safe in our beds again. No more guns. No more bombs or rockets, no more worrying if it was going to be your turn next time the air raid warning sounded. Of course, we let our hair down like never before.

The war was at an end in Europe, and we cherished the normality of peace and an extraordinary feeling of well being, the 'feel good factor' was overwhelming, flooding the souls of those fortunate to survive. The utter hell of it all had suddenly diminished; the fires had stopped burning. There really was a heaven up there. No wonder we sang and danced with joy.

Many of those who lived through those traumatic times, who are still with us these days, will remember how we shared the joy of peace.

Alas, the hopes and dreams of a brave new world did not materialize in the way we would have liked, and many will doubt if the human race will ever learn.

We shall remember those who died, not only in this country but also throughout the world. We may question the peace for which we rejoiced and the ultimate sacrifice at a time when unrest, violence and hatred surround us. We seem to have failed to build that brave new world for their children and grandchildren

But we do have our freedom, and the struggle for peace in the world continues. It must be right for us to give thanks for that, trusting those who have gone before us in the wars did not die in vain. We grow older but we still remember them.

But what did give me hope is, when at the time we were brought up to hate the Germans, was a wonderful story told by my dad after he had been shot down and landed in enemy territory with a parachute. He was captured and treated well in an officer's concentration camp, and he made friends with one of the German guards, quite a different story from many who had rough treatment by the Nazis.

And that qualified my two-and-a-half-year tour with the RAF in Northern Germany after the war, when, stationed as a medic at RAF Rostrup, I met and befriended many Germans who were just like us - which says it all.

The Forties Street Tradesmen

There was never a dull moment in the forties for youngsters in Hampden Road, Harrow Weald. The horrible war had just ended and we enjoyed a wonderful VE (Victory In Europe), street partied in the place we called 'the bend', and we built a bonfire on the site where a house had been. We also burnt an effigy of Hitler to mark the end of that hurt and bloodshed where one of my school friends had been killed with her family after their home had received a direct hit from an enemy bomber. But it was not just the war that killed; it was sometimes the implements of war, like the large steel casement erected to fill with water in case of fire caused by incendiary bombs. Where there's water, kids will play and there seemed to be no provision made for safety or hygiene, one youngster losing his life drowning after having toppled into the six foot deep tank, and others apparently catching diphtheria when the tanks became stagnant.

Soon after safety nets appeared fitted over the tanks and the water changed.

But it was time to rebuild and forget and think of a great new future. Spirits were high and people laughed again. It had been a time when everybody was in the same boat, and many new friendships were made simply, because snobbery and such was generally put aside, because no matter who you were, what your standing, in war you were as vulnerable as the other person.

A big part of my street scene at that time was the regular appearance of the street tradesmen who were abundant, and many had their own brand of humour

Most provisions were carried in horse-drawn carts, and we grew accustomed to the sound of hooves, creaking axles and tradesmen ordering the animals to stop or start with a "woo-back" or "Gee-up."

Some issued the order simply with a "click-click"-sound and shaking the reigns.

Most of the horses seemed quite content and enjoyed the attention of us kids. Sometimes we were allowed to help feed them. We all knew what the sudden raising of the tail meant and quickly retreated while the horse did its business.

And that meant a scurry to collect the droppings for our dads' garden manure, but we compromised to avoid disruptions between us that if a horse did its business in the road directly outside another's house, then that belonged to them. But most times I came up trumps and that meant another tuppence pocket money from my dad when he returned from work later.

The milk came in wide-necked bottles with cardboard tops. There were two different milk companies, the *Express Dairy* and the *United Dairy.* We had the *Express,* and there was always some banter between us as to whose milk tasted the best. In those days, you could really see the cream at the top of the bottle, and I often drank the cream, filled up the bottle again with water and replaced the cardboard top. But, of course, mums are rarely fooled, and I usually got a good telling off later. Sometimes though, when milk had been left on the doorstep when nobody was at home, sparrows and robins and blue tits took to pecking holes in the tops to drink up the cream until people got wise to it and asked the milkman to place Bakelite covers over the bottle tops. In those days, lots of household implements like light switches, lamp holders, torches and radios were made from Bakelite, which was the first type of plastic but very brittle and easily breakable if dropped. The milkman wore a white peaked hat with a white and blue striped cloth apron. When collecting money on Saturdays, his particular vocal sound was instantly recognizable - the rattle of the letter box accompanied by the yodelled cry of "Milko." Of course, he always had a supply of new laid eggs on board, but many of us had our own chickens in those days.

The baker carried a wicker basket full of loaves and cakes. The smell tempted us to go in for the first crusty slice off a new loaf. He knew us well, and we felt he was great, too, because he always had some biscuits to hand out, but occasionally something else. "Look, you are my mates, eh? Tell your mums just how good my angel cake is. Go on have a taster. I've cut a slice 'specially for you!'"

Sure enough, the next time around he would sell off a few of those special angel cakes, which, I remember, were really delicious.

Not so smartly dressed was the Coalman who wore a leather shoulder shield and apron. He always seemed to be broad shouldered and strong, dragging the sacks to the edge of the cart onto his shoulder, bound for the concrete coal cellar in the back garden. It is incredible now to think we used solid fuel to feed our open fires, all those chimneys smoking causing so much of what was called 'smog' when at times you could hardly see a hand stretched out in front of you. Occasionally, if a chimney wasn't regularly swept clean, there would be a chimney fire that always caused a rumpus and excitement watching the firemen do their job. My dad always cleaned his own, which was always fun to watch, waiting for the round brush to appear out of the top of the chimney, me yelling to him that it was through!

Once I heard a thud, a shuffle and a few unmentionable words, my dad appearing as he opened the windows with his face covered in soot and the rest of the living room, too. When cleaning chimneys, a special covering sheet was used with a hole in the middle to ease through the connecting brush rods. It was affixed with strings to hidden bolts on the side supports of the mantelpiece.

I dare not admit that on Guy Fawkes Night I had 'borrowed' the sheet to make a cover over the prepared bonfire, to prevent the rain getting it wet before the big night.

I guess I must have weakened the hole where the string was threaded and that is what caused the accident.

I recall that for months afterwards I felt guilty for not owning up, but it soon passed over. After all, my dad was accustomed to getting soot on his face, being a boiler mechanic in the nearby Kodak factory. I showed off to my mates that my dad was the one who blew the eight-o'clock hooter every weekday morning to alert workers it was time to sign in,

But every time I saw the Coal Delivery man, his face and hands being always covered in coal dust, reminded me of the time of dad's accident, but the whites of his eyes and teeth when he smiled always shone through. His horse was always the most magnificent, a huge animal with leather-blinkered eyes. He was always singing "Old Man River," it seemed, which was a quite popular Paul Robeson song of the time. And he always had that cheery smile for us kids, too.

On summer days, our favourite tradesman came down the road on his tricycle with a large square box at the front. The ice cream man's sound was the ringing of his tricycle bell. We all ran in to collect tuppence and see who would be first back to join the queue.

The ice cream came in round shapes covered with cardboard, which was peeled off. We were jealous of the kids who could afford a choc ice.

My father took up some casual Sunday work with the ice cream vendors. He used to ride his tricycle to Stanmore and traded outside the Hare public house. Once or twice he took me with him, perched on the large box. He always stayed busy on those hot summer days. "You training to go into business with your dad?" was a favourite or "I bet you get 'em free from your dad!"

I will always remember the sound of the Rag and Bone man. His cry was unmistakable, and the whine in his deep haunting voice could be heard from the next road. I guess what he was shouting was "Rag bone, rag bone," though it sounded different. It served to send mums scurrying to see if there was anything they could do without, in return for a reward of a few coppers or a piece of china.

Always scruffy and dirty the Rag and Bone man had holes in his jacket and trousers and wore a greasy peaked hat. But he was always joyful. Even his horse was scruffy. Old sacking was placed over his back and burnt saucepans tied with string around his neck to cause a clatter as he hoofed along the road.

The saddest times were the funerals. It was traditional with some families to invite friends and neighbours to see the deceased before the motorized hearse arrived, to say their final farewells and, perhaps, a small prayer. The youngsters were told to make themselves scarce when the hearse arrived. Curtains were drawn, and men removed their hats in respect.

The *Prudential* insurance man, despite arriving on a very smart bicycle, with clips stopping his trouser turn-ups catching on the chain, was the most posh with that broad, infectious smile and the message that he had got a brand new policy for my mum that she would not want to ignore.

The *Provident* man was popular, too. For the sum of about two pounds per week, which he would regularly collect at the door, one could have a ten-pound loan paid over a number of weeks, which made it seem very attractive and easy to repay. After all, this was big money then and often for our parents out of financial difficulties, especially at Christmas time with all us kids wanting presents.

I can clearly remember tying a big sock on my bed rail, which in the morning would be filled with 'goodies' like fruit and small toys, and then later usually the big toy left by Father Christmas, of course. One year, I was in my element when I got my very first bicycle.

The least popular man to visit the street was the school board man. If we saw him, it usually meant we should be at school. He would arrive on his bicycle when least expected.

Life in the streets was always exiting and interesting. We enjoyed ourselves playing marbles, conkers, skipping, bowling, hoops, hopscotch, and many other games.

Car owners then were in the minority, and they only travelled at about twenty mph, so our street games were rarely disturbed. Only the well off could afford cars; most adults either walked or cycled to work, and, generally, we were a lot fitter then.

Everything seemed so much bigger then, and, of course, there were far less humans on the planet, ironically many having lost their lives in the war.

Our parents worked hard manually to do the regular chores, mum boiling up the gas copper on washday Monday, boiling the whites and hand washing the rest. Sometimes I helped mangling the water out of the clothes before she hung them on a long adjustable washing line, scurrying to bring them in if a sudden shower erupted.

One of my chores was to clean the cutlery on a Sunday morning, else I would have to go to Sunday school!

Then there was the dusting and hand polishing to do all over the house, and with the smoking chimneys there was plenty of that.

But despite all that, it seems to me folk were a lot more contented and happier then, and with the rationing and plenty of manual exercise they were leaner too!

To make ends meet and to feed five of us, including my brothers, my dad took on extra work, like the ice cream selling on a Sunday and repairing clocks and watches in the evenings, while we played indoor games like Ludo, Snakes and Ladders and listened to the 'Wireless,' to the comical genius of Tommy Handley and his ITMA programme, "Take it from here" and "Much Binding in the marsh" and a host more with beloved comedians long gone, but those who helped us through the gravity of war and keep up our spirits.

Peter Pontefract

Peter Pontefract was lost in the snow. Strange how places you know change in the snow.

It covers everything, roads, pavements, signposts; everything is hard to recognize.

Peter told his parents, he wouldn't be long. He was just riding over to see his pal John who lived on the other side of the village. He knew a short cut though the fields.

But who would have reckoned on a severe snowstorm?

He took shelter in a disused barn; the snow was so heavy. When the snowstorm slowed, he went back out. The snow was at least six inches deep. Peter couldn't even see the grass or anything. The hedgerows had disappeared where the wind had drifted the snow against them.

How could he remember which way to go? He knew his way from the barn, but what then? He couldn't see anything but a white mass everywhere.

He couldn't even walk very far because it was so very deep. He was fearful now; it would be dark soon, and what if the snow got even thicker?

Peter Pontefract cried. Lost in the snow, he had nowhere to go. It was also very cold, freezing!

"There must be a way. There has to be a way. I must not cry. I must be brave. Are there such things as snow fairies?" he kept saying to himself.

But snow fairies were for babies. Peter was ten now. No such thing. "Stupid me!"

He heard a rumbling noise in the distance. He looked out of the door. Then the noise stopped. Perhaps it was a snowplough or something clearing the roads. But he could see nothing.

He would wait, that is what he would do. Light a fire from the old wood in the barn. At least he would keep warm and have light when it got dark. After several attempts, he made sparks from rubbing a couple of sticks together. He was glad that his dad had taught him how. He managed to get a fire going with some hay and then putting small pieces of strip wood on top.

He took another quick look outside, just in case. But it was snowing heavily again. He was doing the right thing.

He knew mum and dad would be worrying, so he made up a message to say he was okay in the old barn and not to worry, like a prayer. He hoped that God would pass on the message. If only he had brought his mobile phone!

He heard the strong wind howling, and it seemed the snow was trying to get into the barn, gradually creeping through the cracks in the wood and between the door.

He rubbed his hands together, holding them up to get warmth from the fire. At least he had had tea before he came out, so he wouldn't be hungry for a while. Anyway, he thought, by then the snow will have stopped and someone would be coming to rescue him.

But suddenly there was an almighty gushing sound and the cracking noise of timber. Peter looked up at the roof. The supports had split, and the roof was falling in right over him.

***

The next day, the snowploughs were busy. They had never seen so much snow in the village. It took two hours for the snow ploughs to get through the road leading to the village. Phil and Mary Pontefract were at their wits end. They had heard nothing about their son, Peter.

The local policeman and villagers joined them in the search. But they were looking along the country roads. Peter's parents knew where his pal lived, but they didn't know about the short cut to his house. But then, Peter's pal John remembered. "He probably took the route by the disused barn," he told PC Jones over the telephone.

In a matter of minutes, PC Jones led the villagers including Peter's parents across the field leading to the barn. The local builder, Joe Humphries, cleared a passage through the thick snow with a JCB earth moving mini tractor.

"Oh, my God!" yelled Joe when they got to the barn.

They all looked in horror. The barn had completely caved in, and everything was covered in a fresh fall of snow. Only two of the wooden uprights remained.

"Do you think Peter is under there?" his dad yelled in desperation turning to PC Jones. "It's likely he may have taken shelter there."

PC Jones' expression looked grim. There was no sign of life. No fresh marks in the snow. The whole gathering frantically started to clear the snow and remove the fallen debris but PC Jones urged them to be careful. If

Peter was underneath, they had to be very gentle in shifting the remnants of debris from the roof.

Mary was beginning to lose hope, fearing the worst for her son. "He's not under there. He can't be. There's no sign of life. Please, God, let him be..."

She was unable to complete her sentence; she was so beside herself with anxiety and stress. Phil comforted his wife: "Don't worry. You know Peter. He'd find a way to survive all this."

PC Jones said, it would have helped if there hadn't been a fresh covering of snow. At least then they could have picked up tracks to show whether or not Peter was in the barn.

But then Rick, one of the villagers shouted across: "He's here, he's here, look there's been a fire, there are fresh ashes under melted snow."

"Could have been anyone," replied another, "a tramp or someone."

But Rick continued: "No way! Look it's Peter alright." He pulled Peter's bike up from the debris.

"Oh, my God!" gasped Mary. "That means, he is here, that means..."

They all cleared the area where the fire had been, brushing back the snow with branches stripped from trees. But there was still no sign of Peter.

Rick said, there appeared to be an opening, which had been filled with rocks, but another member of the party, Stan, said that he had worked on the farm in the old days. He knew the barn well, that there was an underground sump beneath the barn to dispose of the water which used to gather there. "No one could survive under that lot," he assured.

Now everybody started to have doubts. Was it going to be a fruitless task? Perhaps, Peter was here but decided to make his way out. He could be anywhere. If he was still alive!

Then somebody heard a dog barking.

"It's Nelly," Phil gasped. "Look, she's attempting to run towards us as if she's trying to tell us something. Look, she's over there, about a hundred meters away."

Joe started the JCB up. There was no time to lose. He started to clear a passage towards Nelly who kept facing them, turning and sniffing what appeared to be a rabbit hole in the snow.

"That's very strange," queried PC. Jones. "There are no tracks in the snow. However did Nelly get here without making tracks?"

"Perhaps she's been there all night," put in Rick. "Perhaps she was with Peter, and he is under there somewhere."

"Afraid not," Phil said glumly. "Nelly has been with us all night at home!"

"That's very strange," said PC Jones, scratching his chin. "No fresh tracks in the snow when there should be, because it hasn't snowed this morning."

"Then there must be a cave or tunnel under here. That is the only answer for it."

"Don't be daft, Phil" ridiculed Stan, "there isn't nothing like that here. I would have known if anyone would. I've ploughed the field and planted cabbages enough times."

"You don't plant cabbages anymore though, do you?" sneered Rick. "You've done much better for yourself, seeing that brand new BMW, you bought. We all wondered how you could afford that."

"That's my business, not yours," replied Stan angrily. PC Jones told them to stop arguing immediately and to put their energies into trying to find the lost boy.

"Let's start digging this out with the JCB" suggested PC Jones. "As there are no dog tracks, there has to be a tunnel or something leading from somewhere. Peter could be trapped inside!"

For some reason Stan didn't want to know. He went marching off, shouting they were on a wild goose chase, and he would look for the boy elsewhere.

PC Jones assumed Stan was behaving like this because of his difference with Rick.

Nelly started to get exited now; her barks were higher pitched. Her tail wagged furiously.

"Good work, Nelly," yelled PC Jones. "Look, there is a tunnel under here, quite a wide one, too. Can you hear me, Peter? Are you there?"

Rick turned to Peter's dad: "That archaeologist was right, Phil. Do you remember several years ago? It was in all the local papers, something about a tunnel leading up from the coast. They reckoned it could have been used by smugglers at one time."

"Of course," Phil said. "It probably led to the barn where the smugglers could hide out until they got transport."

"Shush!" beckoned PC Jones. "I hear something... Yes, a boy's voice... Come down here, Phil. Tell me if that's the voice of your son."

Phil listened intensely. He heard the voice. It was like a radio on low volume. He could just make out the words.

"I'm here, where the old stile leading down to Reebs cove is. I'm at the end of the tunnel. I can't move because I'm trapped behind a rock at the opening."

There were shouts of joy. "It's Peter!" cried Phil. The sad expression on Mary's face changed instantly to that of relief. Peter was alive, thank God.

When they got to where Peter had directed, they saw a foot appearing behind rocks. The JCB gradually pulled them away until they were able to free Peter. There was hardly a bruise on him.

Peter told his dad, there was someone outside minutes before they arrived, because he had nearly freed himself from the tunnel - that's how he could see where he was - but the man came up from behind, pushed him back into the tunnel and laid some heavy rocks back over the entrance.

He didn't see who he was. He was a very big man. And, another thing... When the roof of the barn came down, he discovered the tunnel under the barn, which had been opened by the falling debris. Also, just inside were hoards if glittering things like diamond necklaces and things.

"So that's what happened to them," smiled PC. Jones. "Remember the big jewel robbery a year ago in Hempsham? We have never been able to trace the stolen jewels. But it seems as though we have now. At the time, we thought there must have been some local interest and from Stan's behaviour today I wouldn't be at all surprised if he is involved,"

"So that's how he could afford all those expensive things, like that BMW and everything," put in Rick. " I never trusted him from the start. His eyes looked a bit shifty to me."

"Still, thank heaven, you are okay, Peter," smiled PC. Jones. "We noticed, your bike was a write-off, though."

PC Jones was right. Immediately after saying goodbye to Peter and his parents and thanking everybody for their help in finding the boy, he made tracks for the barn. He discovered Stan fanatically trying to save the stolen jewels and to hide them somewhere else before the police arrived. But the snow prevented him from doing that. It was proved, Stan was one of the main burglars and was keeping the jewels stashed away until it was safe to dispose of them for cash.

Young Peter was famous. Everybody wanted to talk to him about his great adventure and how he found the lost jewels. The local newspaper bought him a brand new mountain bike.

He was glad, he took the short cut after all on that cold wintry day, but he would never take chances again, at least not without checking the weather forecast first.

A Page Out of Marcus's Book

It was the end for Marcus and Rebecca Cohen. The focus of that which was once part of their lives remained the broken walls and the scattered belongings of their home for fifty years. Billows of black smoke arose from the pile in Green Street, Harrow Weald. Books and other items tumbled from the crumbling shelves and cupboards. Book bindings ripped in the blast like tissue paper, pages floating like autumn leaves and settling on the dusty debris.

It was 1944. A German Heinkel bomber, having released its bombs a moment before it crashed, exploded in field adjacent to the Cohen's home, but it seemed a bomb scored a direct hit on the semi-detached house.

An RAF Spitfire fighter aircraft circled above. The young Canadian pilot watched in horror. He had targeted the Heinkel successfully, aimed to bring it down out of harm's way in the open fields of Harrow Weald, and taking his life into his hands; his guns had blazed at the rudder, attempting to divert the Bomber. But it was to no avail as it spiralled almost vertically to the built up area below.

It had all gone terribly wrong. He prayed, hope against hope, that nobody was hurt.

For a brief moment, he was in his element. Playing the part so courageously fought by his predecessors in The Battle of Britain, to destroy the enemy at all cost. But now he turned his nose for return to Northolt base. He felt drained. If only he had left the bloody thing alone. It was just another ego trip, another hit to chalk up. But it was another feather in his cap; it was an enemy craft, another score to his list of seven. That was the job he did - but what of the consequences?

"You did what you knew was right, Dave," the squadron officer assured when, after touch down, Dave filed his report. "The chips were down, old chap. If you hadn't shot the bastard down he'd have dropped his bombs and possibly killed someone anyway. That's the name of the game. Now go and get some shuteye. Don't want my pilots overdoing it."

But in moments, Dave was in his MG driving to the stricken scene. He had to know the outcome.

The debris was still smouldering profusely; there were small fires everywhere. One house was completely demolished, save one wall and staircase. On the wall and over a mantel over the fireplace a mirror hung precariously, but miraculously still intact. And what looked like a cupboard area below the stairway was also still in one piece. Perchance those survivors were still there, tucked inside?

Two helpers appeared from behind a mound of debris. They carried a stretcher. Then two defense workers followed with another stretcher. Dave saw in horror the two bodies were motionless. He stumbled to his knees in despair: "I'm sorry. I am so sorry. Please forgive me!"

A young woman stood alone like she was frozen, tears in her eyes.

"Who were they?" Dave asked.

"They were my neighbours, " she replied. "I was only speaking to them earlier when I asked if they wanted any shopping. They were a smashing couple; they just didn't deserve such an abrupt ending to their lives at their age. Marcus and Rebecca Cohen they were. Jewish, you know. You'd think they'd have been safe from old Hitler over here. Joy is going to be heartbroken."

"Joy?" Dave enquired.

"She's their daughter, working away in Lincolnshire in the land army."

The bodies gone, somehow Dave was drawn to the mirror over the mantelpiece and clambered awkwardly over the debris. Standing there, struggling to keep a balance on the moving debris, he focused into the mirror, imagining reflections of the past, of Marcus and Rebecca, how life must have been for them before he wrecked it all. He felt he wanted to put that to rights, but how? The past is the past and cannot be undone; he only hoped if there was a God they would forgive him in that next world.

He thought he saw something, but shook his head. His mind was playing tricks. Simply that. He looked away to gather his foothold on the sliding debris. Life had to carry on. Then whatever pulled him back to stare into the mirror made him gasp. The images he saw were still there, as if recorded and implanted in the mirror forever, gazing back at him, a suggestion of a smile on a woman's face but not on the man's. He felt strangely compelled to concentrate, focusing his all into the mirror. He felt he was being pulled into another time, passing through the mirror like a spiral. He heard a voice, a woman's voice...

***

"Marcus, awaken yourself. Must I always fight to bring you back to life?"

38

Marcus groaned, snorted and stretched his legs across the stool supporting them.

Opening his eyes, he saw Rebecca standing over him and felt the pressure of her hand rubbing his shoulder, her silver-grey hair glowing as her head eclipsed the streaming rays of sunlight through the window.

"What now, Rebecca? Can't a man snooze in his own armchair by his own fire? What have I done already to deserve such treatment from my loving wife?"

Rebecca looked down at the balding head of her husband, a few strands of grey hair remaining. She still saw the face of a younger man, the man she had fallen for many years before. She turned towards the mirror above the mantelpiece pointing a finger.

"Look into the mirror, Marcus. Tell me what you see."

Marcus groaned. "You awaken me to see what's in the mirror?"

"Shush, just look," Rebecca urged.

"I see nothing, what am I supposed to see? What does anyone see in a mirror? A reflection."

"I see the face of a sad young man in the RAF uniform. He has wings sewn on his jacket. A pilot. Marcus. Who do we know is an RAF pilot?"

"We know no RAF pilots, dear. You must be seeing things. If you really see the reflection, then he is here with us, in this room!"

"Did Joy say, she had a new boyfriend?" queried Rebecca. "Perhaps it is him."

"You are crazy, Rebecca. Who would come here? Joy is in Lincolnshire farming the land for victory."

"Look, he has picked up the book from the mantelpiece, he opens it at our page," Rebecca whispered excitedly. "You know what we must do!"

"It is rude to point, Rebecca, so you always tell me," yawned Marcus. "Anyway, I am much too tired to look. Nobody has turned to our page since the year dot."

"Marcus, you old fox. You complain, nobody turns to our page. Now somebody has you think of sleep! What must I do to make you pay attention? Mama Mia!"

"I told you, Rebecca, don't say that. You are not an Italian but a good English Jew like your husband. So why say Mama Mia?"

"Marcus, don't try your old tricks again to distract my attention. Why did you take the job? You chose to be a fictitious character, convinced me to join you. Look, he begins to read, listen, he reads aloud, he reads of you!"

"Marcus Cohen snoozed in his armchair beside a roaring fire." The voice seemed far away.

"Do you hear, Marcus? We must do something, anything. What is so interesting about Marcus and his wife in this predicament? The reader will expect some kind of action else he will put the book down. Kiss me or something, give him romance!"

"Rebecca, I'm too old for that!"

"You were too old in life. So what's new? Be sensible, Marcus."

Marcus quickly got up to take a closer look into the mirror, knocking over the footstool.

He frowned. "That's a man?"

"Marcus, look he has whiskers. Would a woman have whiskers?"

"My mother did!"

"Your mother, your mother. You make her sound like an ape. You should respect her now. She's gone to that other place. She didn't have to hang about like we do, suspended in a void. We have unfinished business on earth we are told, but what, I don't know."

Marcus looked again into the mirror, closer. He stood up and smiled the smile of a man attracted by a woman.

"That is definitely no man!" he reinstated. "That is a woman. No man has those womanly blue eyes, lips like that and the soft tint in the hair, which deliciously droops below her chin. That is a she!"

"I think we are both seeing different people, dear. I see an RAF pilot!" Rebecca was adamant.

"I tell you, 'he' is a she," Marcus insisted.

"Well, at least this reader is making you pay attention, so I will go along with you. It will provide action maybe. Look the reader's eyes are wandering, quick, provide some dramatics!"

"To be or not to be," started Marcus.

"Not to be," interrupted Rebecca. "If the reader wanted Shakespeare, she would be reading Shakespeare. Look! Now the hands are pressing the book. I expect she grows tense. We must provide some action. Remember your vows. On earth you claimed never to have done good, and you wished to make up for that. You chose to be a fictitious character to give others the impression that you are a wonderful man who, by his own actions, would endeavour to impress the reader, to give pleasure and enjoyment to all who read of you and your wife."

"But is has all been done before," groaned Marcus. "Don't you see?"

"If it has, it has, Marcus. What difference does it make?"

"I wanted to be exclusive. You want to know the real reason I took this job to make good for my earthly sins? Nobody would want to read about me. They would probably say: 'Marcus Cohen, who is he anyway?' A couple of paragraphs and that's it. The reader is bored, so what does he do? He closes the book, and I go back to my snoozing."

"Marcus Cohen! If you were not a good Jew on earth then be a good Jew in spirit now. One of mankind's greatest inspirations was literature. Now you have the power to be somebody. You have the power to be good in some way, no matter how small. Why must you speak the way you do?"

"I told you, Rebecca, no matter what, we are just a figment of the author's imagination. We can only do that which the author commands us to do. I want do to do what I want to do. I want to have freedom to do just that!"

"How can you say that? You know, we came to life in the author's mind at the stroke of a pen. Many author's support the view that the characters come to life in a sense and to some extent, seem to control the imagination of the author. Take William Shakespeare for instance. Could any one man write so well without the spirit we are able to transmit? His characters come to life like the canvass of a brilliant painter, the works of a great composer. You think they had no help from beyond? Sometimes you speak a lot of nonsense, Marcus. Sometimes I wish I had chosen to spend my spiritual life with Joe. He was inventive, and he was brilliant!"

"Then why did you not marry him on earth?"

"Because, Marcus Cohen, I loved you. Because I …shush, our reader seems to be trying to attract our attention. The pilot has gone. It is now a young lady!"

"I told you so, Rebecca. She is talking to us, she is…"

"Oh Marcus, Rebecca, you must be my grandparents. I can see and hear you as I read. You seem real. Our home is how I remember father's description. Listen to me if you are real. Look into the page and see yourselves in your familiar surroundings. I'm not frightened because I know who you are."

Marcus and Rebecca looked into the mirror but their eyes and actions were frozen.

"Don't be concerned. It's okay. I am your granddaughter. My name is Susan. I'm now twenty years old, so you won't know me. I can see you. It's wonderful, all those old fashioned surroundings, just how they were in the forties. Tell me it's not my imagination, please. Please answer me. You can hear and see, can't you?"

Rebecca's stare softened. She turned excitedly to Marcus.

"See our reader speaks to us. We give pleasure."

But her old eyes saw only a blur, and Marcus had difficulty to focus. Images were disappearing.

Marcus gasped. "Oh God in heaven, she is talking to us. But how can it be? Susan, Susan, I hear you. I hear my granddaughter speaking to me!"

Tears were streaming down his cheeks.

"Shush! The voice starts again. Another voice." Rebecca nudged Marcus.

"Rebecca, I am your daughter, Joy. If you cannot see me, listen. I wrote a true story of you, my parents, in the fifties. You are fact, not fiction."

"Marcus, I am so excited," yelled Rebecca. "I hear the voice of our daughter speaking to us. She is out there. Through the mirror she knows our spirits exist."

"Rebecca, this is getting complicated. You hear our daughter but I can only hear our granddaughter, Susan. Wait, you see what happens when I speak to her. Susan, read on until you come to a blank area, so the lines of words do not hide you from us."

"Grandpa, Grandpa! You can hear me?"

"Yes, I can hear you. Don't cry, we are both fine. Rebecca, say hello to our granddaughter."

"But Marcus, all I can see is a blur, but I hear the voice of our daughter. Isn't it wonderful?"

"Rebecca, we are both hearing different members of our family simultaneously. But wait, wait! I begin to see her clearly again. She is beautiful."

"I also see the face of our daughter!" gasped Rebecca. "It's as if I have been given new eyes. She is very much like you, Marcus, her voice, her features, she reminds me of ..." But she sees the images begin to fade and the voices quieted.

"Grandpa, many of the older generation remember you and grandma in the little grocery store. During those harsh war years they remember you for your cheer and good spirits. I will keep this book forever."

Marcus was overwhelmed. "Susan says, we are remembered. We have both left our mark, Rebecca."

"Well, your daughter has written a book about you, dear. Does that not prove your worth on earth?"

"You are right, Rebecca. As usual you are right!"

Marcus collapsed heavily in his armchair and was soon in deep, deep sleep.

"Marcus Cohen," cried Rebecca, "you are sleeping again."

"No, I will not awaken you this time," she added. "Perhaps our time here is complete."

Rebecca quietly sat down and started her knitting, but soon she too was in deep slumber.

Neither heard the whining of the air-raid siren. In minutes they were like embers of the past. Life was no more.

***

Dave Turner, the Canadian pilot, returned to his homeland with an English wife when the war was over. He was now in his sixties. Sadly, his wife died early but they had a daughter, Jenny. She married an Englishman and was now living in London.

It was 1999. The time was now ripe for Dave to return to London for a vacation. Jenny insisted he should stay with them. He had lived with the silent memory of the war and still felt responsible for the death of Marcus and Rebecca Cohen. He wanted to know more about them and what happened to their daughter, Joy.

He visited the scene of the bombing in Harrow Weald. He remembered the road, but the row of Victorian houses had gone. An office block stood where Marcus and Rebecca once lived.

He stood motionless, visualizing the scene when last he was there. It was a cloudy spring day but, occasionally, the sun broke through and shafts of bright light caught the large windowpanes reflecting sparkles of scattered prisms of light upon his car.

Dave squinted to see the scene. For a brief moment he saw a mirror on the wall in one of the offices, clearly visible though the large windows.

He attempted to focus on the mirror and even although it was far away, he visualized the images he remembered only too well. But he had to get nearer. Was his mind playing tricks again?

Dave loved flying, and he still flew most days in his Cessna, a little different though than when having gained his wings in the RAF. He was soon put onto Spitfires and even now the sound of those Merlin engines still rung in his ears. His dream to fly a Spit had come true. He called it his sugar baby and being one of the fortunate ones, it saw him through that ghastly war.

He recalled thinking, what a way to live, zooming upwards into the clouds, spinning, diving, looping the loop. It was all so easy in that beautiful manoeuvrable sugar baby.

He was going to show those Limeys what a Canic could do; that is what the Brits called him, Canic. As far as he was concerned, armed with his sugar baby, the enemy did not stand one iota of a chance, and he soon claimed seven hits.

But then his mind drifted hearing the unique sound of bomb filled Heinkel bombers overhead, and the call from HQ to intercept. And once more that awful feeling of guilt came over him, the horrendous sight of that bomber hurtling to the ground.

How he remembered one of his colleagues having shot down one of the new German revenge weapons, the flying bomb nicknamed the 'Doodlebug' and how he, unfortunately, had similarly caused a direct hit into a block of houses.

There he was again, going for that Hun, perforating the tail rudder and watching it dive down. And then a flash below, and it was done. Hit number eight. But what of the consequences!

But then, there was another flash. He was back here in the present, shattered office windows flying in all directions. He felt the blast push him rigidly against a wall and then darkness...

Coming to, he saw a paramedic leaning over him.

"What the hell was that?" Dave yelled, "Was it a bomb?"

"Some sort of gas explosion," the medic replied. "Fortunately, the office was empty. Don't worry, you will be fine, just a gash on the forehead, that's all. No problem."

How odd that could happen within yards of the spot of that ghastly disaster when Marcus and Rebecca met their end.

Dave had to put it down to coincidence.

The next day Dave decided to pay a visit to the local library seeking a report on that day of the bombing in Green Street but his efforts were in vain. Looking at a map singling out every bombing in Harrow that year, there was no reference to the Marcus and Rebecca address, just a mention that an enemy aircraft had crashed nearby.

As he looked through the records, he felt a presence and looked up to see a kind smiling face of a woman approximately his age.

"You are Canadian, aren't you?" she asked, and as if sensing a query in Dave's expression she continued. "I caught your accent when you were at the counter. I'm the librarian here. I see you have an interest in wartime Britain and wondered if I could help. You look a little bit lost."

He was taken by her; her aura was warm, welcoming.

"I guess, you are right on both counts," Dave replied. "I was stationed over here during the war with the RAF at nearby Northolt."

He felt reluctant to offer any further information. He obviously wasn't proud of shooting down a German bomber killing civilians, yet he felt there was a possible link, and the librarian may possibly be able to solve. So he would lightly enquire.

"I was a pilot, and I am doing some research on enemy bombings is the vicinity during the war," he continued.

He saw the librarian's face stiffen. Had he said the wrong thing? Was he bringing something up of the past best forgotten? Just maybe, it was his guilty conscience at work again.

She smiled again. "We are arranging a gathering here next week, sights and sounds of the war years locally, to give an insight to those who did not experience how it was in Harrow during the war. There is a lot of interest at the moment, and I feel sure your contribution would be invaluable."

But Dave looked apprehensive.

"Perhaps you would like to come? There will be ample refreshments, and one of our members makes a mean apple and blueberry pie, which I know you Canadians love."

Dave put on a smile. "You know how to tempt me."

He had to face up to the truth, and he felt sure there would now be no animosity given the passing of time, that he was just doing his job.

"Then you will come. I am so pleased. My name is, by the way, Joy Cohen."

"Dave Turner." He shook Joy's hand warmly. Was this another coincidence, the librarians name being Joy Cohen, could she be the daughter of … he'd ask, he could only ask, his eagerness for information had already opened up more conversation;

"You were in the land army during the war, right, Joy?"

Joy's expression showed surprise. Dave could sense the pondering of her thoughts. He had to be open, he must know at all costs. He needed forgiveness for his 'big mistake.'

If she was the daughter, who better maybe to ease his conscience? But would she be bitter and repel him? He had to know.

"You have to be the Canadian pilot who came to apologise. Marcus and Rebecca Cohen were my parents. I remember their neighbour telling me about you."

"Yes, I am the pilot. I'm sorry. I did try to avert the bomb."

"You don't have to be sorry. I have been trying to contact you for years, having heard of your concern, but couldn't find out your name. You were not responsible for their deaths. It was later confirmed the death of my parents was caused by a gas leak moments before the bomb hit. It actually exploded some distance away in the field at the back of my parents' garden, near to where the plane came down, too. After all these years, some fifty-five years ago now, there emerged another gas leak causing a minor explosion, thank goodness. It has come to light that there is some sort of subsidence going on, which caused a fracture in the gas supply, and they are presently installing new pipes."

"I will definitely be coming to your gathering, Joy. Thanks for everything. You just don't know what this means to me."

Dave felt that the cross he had to bear for so long, had gone forever.

"You must come round this weekend and meet the family, Dave. They would love to meet you."

When Dave took up the invitation and visited Joy's home, and after the introductions to her husband and two children, he saw the mirror and instantly knew it had belonged to Joy's parents. It was over another mantelpiece in another place in another time, but he could still feel and sense the aura.

"Look into the mirror," Joy urged. "What do you see?"

"I see myself and the happy family of Marcus and Rebecca. The reflections of the past are replaced by those of the present. Indeed, a real joy to behold."

46

History Rules

Val responded to the bleep on her mobile phone. It was Rick, sounding frantic. But lately that was nothing new. She just wanted him out of her hair.

They had been living together for just two years. It all started so well, them getting a flat together and Rick being forever the considerate guy he was. A self-employed decorator, he did a splendid job redecorating the tenancy, which made so much difference to their lives after having moved into a pigsty of a place, but getting it on a cheap rent, they didn't argue. With the woman's touch, some scrubbing and cleaning there, some tidying here and Rick's busy paint brush to the fore came a few sheets of wallpaper. The place looked so very much different and fit to live in once again. So just what happened to this once so in love couple?

"Are you calling from Morrison's, Rick? I thought you couldn't make personal calls from work!"

"This is urgent, Val. Alright if I pop around tonight? Something I must say."

"Say it now, Rick. I've got a hot date tonight."

"I can't tell you on the mobile. I have to tell you face to face."

"Okay, Rick but make it quick. Look, I must hang up. I am changing Laura's nappy. What's that? Yes, come at seven, that's fine."

On the dot of seven, Rick was at Val's place. She had made up her mind, there would be no hanging around: "Look, Rick I've got to go. Barbara is looking after the little lady. Wish she would stop crying."

Rick looked bemused by his late partner's attitude. It was so unlike her. Even to let him see his daughter occasionally was a headache. And he still didn't know exactly what he had done to turn her against him so much, the girl he cherished and still loved despite all.

"That's what babies do, cry!" Rick was being pedantic.

"And how would you know? You know nothing. Sometimes I really wish I had never met you."

Val was flushed and getting near hysterical. That is how Rick seemed to be affecting her of late.

"Then there would be no Laura, so I do have my uses."

47

"Did! Let's make that perfectly clear, Rick. I told you already, we are finished. There are only two important people in my life, Laura and Joe. So get that into your head once and for all!"

"But I loved you, and I still do, Baby. Doesn't that mean anything to you?"

"We were fine until you got yourself into trouble running that doomed decorating business. You should have realised, with Laura coming along, that we needed every penny. But you? You try and show off and go for the big jobs and not having the business sense, you thinking you knew it all, refusing that business course offered you by the social. You had no idea how to run big business, and now look at you!"

"Well, I have a job. Okay, it is only supermarket shelf filling but I will do better, I promise. Laura is my child, too. You seem to forget that!"

"Well, you should have thought of that when you went onto drugs. There - you thought I didn't know, didn't you? That is where all your hard earned money went and then losing out on your business too, it was just too much, I could see where it was all going, and I didn't want any part of it, and neither will your daughter."

"Look, Val," Rick was pursued. "Will you please just sit? Give me just five minutes, that's all. I realise my faults and aim to mend them, just another chance is all I want, and, anyway, there is something I have to tell you. So will you just listen for one minute? That's all I ask of you."

She obeyed, but reluctantly, still doing her make-up, looking very stiff-lipped like she had no intention of budging one iota. Since the rift came, Val had come to terms with herself, considering always what she thought best for Laura. It had knocked her sideways when she discovered drugs in Rick's trouser pocket, but it only confirmed what she had been suspecting for some time, just the smell of him, his clothes, that certain smell of cannabis she had read so much about of late. And then what messed it for once and for all was the police drug raid, when they barged though the front door and set Laura off screaming, and arresting Rick into the bargain.

"What sort of father are you? How could you? I just don't want anything more to do with you," she yelled hysterically as the police took him out.

Twisting and turning, he twisted himself around in the narrow space of the doorway, wedging himself there, making it difficult for the police to pull him through, yelling to Val to please forgive him, but although he attempted to free himself, the police would have none of it and securely handcuffed him, leaving Val's baby Laura in her arms, screaming and crying.

He got six months suspended sentence on good behaviour and a £200 fine.

Now, as Rick attempted still to seek forgiveness, Val looked up at the strong square jaw of the guy she once thought she loved, and his eyes told her he wanted her. Momentarily, her mindset was in the not so distant past, they would fall out big time, yes, although in her eyes he seemed to make nothing of it. And that was always the problem with Rick, he was so casual about things, important things like keeping up with the rent to name but one. She had finished her make-up and felt really good. No way was Rick going to spoil her evening.

"There's something you must know, Val. Something very urgent. Something serious that affects you and Joe."

"Are you, serious, Rick? Come off it. That is so uncharacteristic. You were never that, and that's been the problem all along. Okay, as you said, you've got to have a sense of humour, but some things in life just need to be taken seriously, and that is where you have miserably failed, Rick."

All that was in Val's mind was that Rick would never give up trying in vain to smooth things over, to make alright what just never would be alright again. She had had it up to here. She was about to be blatantly rude, if that was to be the only way, but she would give him the time he wanted, just this once.

"Rick, you will never change my mind. I know, we were an item once and then Laura materialised. But with Joe... What can I say? He's a great find. Next to Laura he is my life now."

"But are you sure, you really want to be with him, that you really love him as a woman loved a man and not ..."

"Look, what sort of person do you think I am? You talk as though I am mentally disturbed, like I don't know my own mind. Joe is a guy who can make two of you, and he has real consideration, too."

"But no matter what, I will always be Laura's father, and you owe it to me to either give me a second chance or let me see her regularly."

"So you can punch Joe in the nose, just for being here. Like you said, that you could never bear the thought of any other being in my bed. Well, if it is anything to you, Joe has been in my bed."

"You slut, you bloody slut," Rick yelled. "You have the gall to sleep in our bed! How does that make you feel or are you some sort of pervert about that?"

"Why is it that some guys always call a woman that when, if they only knew, it was love? I happen to love Joe as I said a dozen times already, and I aim to marry him. And if it is of any condolence, I have a new bed, a new mattress, everything. Okay?"

Rick stood there, realising what he had said. There he was aiming to pick up the pieces, knowing that when Val found out the truth about Joe, that she could never ever marry him, let alone sleep with him, and now what made it worse was that she already had. How would she feel now when she discovered the truth?

"You are making it harder for me, Val. But I'll be around to pick up the pieces, if that is what you want. You just said you aim to marry Joe, but take it from me, there is absolutely no way, and you know something? You never ever asked me that!"

"You never asked, Rick, so come off it! For me, marriage is how it should be. Once I believed it was right for us and longed for you to ask the question. I hinted enough!"

Val was getting tenser by the second. *He must think, he owns me. What a ...*

Her thoughts were disturbed by Rick's raised voice. "So you bloody well have slept with him, you have now admitted that."

If looks could kill, Val's were lethal.

"Don't look at me like that," he yelled, "It's important. I must know, if I'm no longer your lover, I'm still your friend, even just for Laura's sake. I told you, I will always be her dad, and you can't change that, ever. I still want you to be happy, and Joe just has to be a wimp."

"What's it with you, Rick, asking me that? I love him. Don't you understand? We are meant for each other, simply that. End of story."

"Sorry to tell you, but not quite, I have something that will stop you from wanting Joe that way."

"Look, you poor misguided twit," Val was in tears now. "Who are you to judge and attempt to stop me from seeing the new guy in my life, a guy who really does want to make a serious issue of our relationship? He really cares for me in a way you never could."

"Absolutely, you are dead right, Val. I could never love you as a brother!"

"What?"

50

"You and Joe can never be right for each other like that. I'm researching family histories and by chance clicked into yours. It's all on the net, Val. Joe is your brother, your full brother by blood, see!"

Val's face dropped.

Now she was really angry. She was almost hysterical. "You really will try anything, won't you, Rick? You just never give up, do you? Just pee off, go. Get out of my life."

"Okay, Val. But remember my offer. I shall always be there for you. And I still love you, for God's sake!"

In the next day's post Val received a printout of her family history with just the words "Sorry, Val" scribbled on top.

She knew that her dad died with T.B. when he was only twenty-one, but she didn't know about Joe.

Two years after dad's passing, her mother remarried and had another son. But Val and Joe must have been too young to know.

On further enquiries Val discovered her mother and stepfather couldn't afford to keep the three kids, so poor Joe had to go. He was adopted at the early age of two.

In the end Val had to be philosophical. After all she had gained a brother.

And she hadn't slept with Joe. It was all a story to be rid of Rick forever.

But as for Rick… End of story.

The Christmas of 43

"Your cat's got nine lives. You haven't!"

It was that darned air raid precaution warden again, calling at our door, yelling we had a beam of light coming from our front window. Ironically, we could have told him it was the cat's fault.

In the war after sunset, when we needed to put on our lights indoors, we had to make sure windows were completely blacked out should there be an air raid. If the German bombers spotted a shaft of light it would give them a pointer to drop their bombs. That was the theory anyway, and air raid precaution wardens were employed to ensure no light was showing. One could be prosecuted for abuse of this wartime regulation.

I was just eleven years old in 1943. In North London Hitler had been pretty hard on us, relentlessly and indiscriminately bombing all and sundry, and his ruthless bombers were droning overhead it seemed nearly every night. Mum wanted my brother and I evacuated, but we played up so much, she decided against it, and with Dad being away in the war, and she only otherwise having Tibby the cat for company, I guess helped her change her mind.

We were quite happy of course living at home with Mum and Tibby, too. He was my pet marmalade cat. I loved him deeply. He was a great comfort with dad being away and the stress poor Mum was going through. She was expecting an addition to the family just after Christmas. She said, I would have to be the man of the house while Dad was away to keep an eye on my seven-year-old brother, John.

"Now is the time for you to be really brave, Peter, with Hitler and all those nasty bombs coming down."

Looking back, our parents really had a rough deal in those days with everything on ration and poor old Mum having to scrimp and scrape to keep my brother and me fed and happy. But she always managed to keep our bellies full, regardless. And what she could do with a couple of bones from the butchers was sheer magic, those stews I can still taste and her suet puddings were the tops. We lived on old-fashioned porridge oats for breakfast, the type you had to simmer and stir until cooked, and I often got that job. And come tea time, it was dripping and winkles and bread and butter, and I can still remember removing the caps with a pin of those winkles and dipping them in salt.

Given the shortages at Christmas, you'd have thought Mum could get nothing for the Christmas table, but somehow she did, and given the dining room ceiling almost obscured by those gummed paper chains us kids made, we enjoyed the sheer luxury of a home reared chicken, and her carrot cakes were a real treat.

I felt protective of my mum. I didn't like the warden talking to her like that, the night the air raid siren bellowed out once again. It seemed it went off every night of late.

"Put that bloody light out," he said. "This is the second time I have had to warn you. Those Jerry's up there, if they see your light they'll drop a bomb right on your bloody head. And blow us all to smithereens!"

I joined my mum at the front door and yelled at him. "It's Tibby, our cat. He just likes to jump up and claw the blackout at the window. Don't blame my mum!"

That is when he said it. "Your cat's got nine lives. You haven't. Keep the cat away from the windows."

I tried to act grown up, and thought of what Dad would say in this situation. Dad was always so calm and placid.

"I guess he's only doing his job, Mum," I said afterwards.

Mum disagreed, though. She said, he wasn't really interested in our welfare, but in the power that stupid ARP helmet gave him. I discovered earlier that ARP stood for Air Raid Precaution, and our warden, Jack Bray, happened to be our neighbour, too. She had never seen eye to eye with him since two weeks before when he had grumbled about us having chickens in the garden. He complained about their crowing in the early hours after he had been on late duty.

I was proud of our chickens. I had built the chicken house and the run with old timber. Lots of people were encouraged to keep them during the war when food was short. We always had fresh eggs.

I noticed, Mum kept on about Jack the warden. He was getting to her, and she hated him. So did I then for upsetting her. Next time I saw him in the street, I knocked his helmet off and ran away. But he had the last laugh. The milkman's horse drawn cart had just been around, and I tripped and landed in some horse dung. I hated him all the more now; there was no getting back at him.

When the air raid warning sounded, we all made for the Anderson shelter in the back garden. It was built of corrugated curved strips covered in earth, which was dug out to make a pit for the base of the shelter. It made for good protection, and many lives in the war were saved because of them. Another option was the 'Morrison' shelter, which came in sheets of brown steel plate with steel legs and a ribbed steel cage and was built usually in the living room when a quick escape from the danger of bombing could effectively be made. But our Anderson version was quite comfy, kitted out with bunks, a small stove and even 'poes,' as we called them, a small steel receptacle for toilet arrangements. During those dark days, they were used in the home, too, usually because toilets were built outside.

Sometimes we spent the night down in the shelter when the air raids became frequent. I made sure Tibby was with me.

I remember one could always tell when the German bombers above were fully loaded by the tone of the engine. Once dropped, the tone lightened as they turned back to their home base. We could hear the bombs whistling down and prayed they would miss us. I clearly remember being frightened to death as a string of bombs came down around us, two directly hitting a house a few yards down our road, killing my school friend and his parents and another two landing in the fields behind us with a horrendous thud and explosion which seemed to go on forever.

One evening, a week prior to Christmas, we made for the shelter as there were reports that another heavy raid was imminent. But I couldn't find Tibby. I was devastated and told Mum I would have to go and find him. But the air raid siren had already sounded, and we could hear the German bombers approaching in the distance. Mum told me to stay put. A bomb crashed down quite close to us. The noise was dreadful, and the earth shook violently. All I could think of was Tibby. Then, mercifully, the "all clear" siren sounded. But I soon had something else to occupy my mind.

I heard Mum groaning. "Peter, you will have to run to the telephone box. The new baby is coming early!" she cried. "Here's the number to ring."

Now I really had to act grown up. Mum was depending on me, and she handed me a piece of notepaper. I clambered out of the shelter and made for the telephone box just on the corner of our road and shouted to anyone I saw: "Help! My mum is having a baby!"

I rushed back after I got through to the midwife to see how Mum was. I was relieved when I saw the warden's wife from next-door attending to Mum. She was a nurse, fortunately, and said she had heard my calls coming from the bottom of our garden where the shelter was situated. She asked me to take my brother back to the house.

In the morning when I awoke, Mrs. Bray stood by my bed with a mug of tea in her hand. She gave it to me and said my mum was in her bedroom. She said, she was okay, and I had got a brand new brother. I was so relieved and happy, until I thought of Tibby.

"I don't suppose you have seen our cat, Tibby?" I asked.

"Afraid not, Peter, but don't worry. He'll be alright, you just wait and see. Cats have got nine lives you know."

I couldn't wait to see Mum and the new baby. He was great and Mum looked so radiantly happy. "Dad will be surprised when he comes home, won't he, Mum?"

"I'm sure he will. Let's hope that will be soon, Peter. It's been six months since he's been away. Now I can see you are longing to go and search for Tibby, aren't you? Run along then. I will be fine. But do be careful of the debris."

Because of the bombing close by, many windows had been shattered, and there was glass everywhere, but already hoards of volunteers were clearing it up and cheering themselves with big mugs of tea and sing-songs. That is how it was in those days. The motto was to 'keep your chin up' and be happy. I will always remember the great spirit of the grownups. They were all in the same boat, and it was everybody helps each other. And generally it seemed to work, and moral was kept generally high despite the horrors of war.

I searched and searched, but could not find Tibby. I was beginning to fear the worst, and tears were in my eyes when I returned home. It had been a terrifying day, a joyful day being presented with a new brother, and a sad day all rolled into one.

Later in the evening, there was a knock at the door. Looking at the glass screen in the top of the door I recognised the ARP warden's helmet. I thought the worst, glanced at the blackout but it was alright. I would be ready for him. I opened the door, stood my ground, and faced him. It was Jack Bray from next door.

"I think this moggy belongs to you," he said, cradling Tibby in his arms. "Afraid, he was trapped in the debris of the house that was hit down the road last night. It's okay. He's alright. Good job we found him, though. I guess, he's only got six lives left now."

"Five." I corrected, adding: "He nearly suffocated once when he got stuck up the chimney!"

Although Tibby looked ragged and dirty, he warmed in my arms when Jack Bray handed him carefully to me and rubbed the end of his nose to mine.

"I think, I detect a purr there, Peter," he said with a smile. I was still very young, but the lesson learned was the man I had hated so much was now one of the best, and I realized, I owed so much for what he and his wife had done.

I don't think we could have coped that Christmas without our kindly neighbours, especially as it was our first without Dad. After that, Mum regularly gave our neighbours some of our newly laid eggs, which seemed to solve the problem about the noisy chickens.

"Guess you were right, Peter," Mum said the following morning. "I mean what you said about Jack the warden just doing his job. Just goes to show, you can't tell a man by his helmet. And who'd have thought his wife Sheila was a nurse once. And, by the way, the postman has just delivered a letter. Look, Dad will be home for the New Year!"

I shall always remember the Christmas of 43.

The Demise of Florence Harper

In the summer of 1864, Florence Harper found employment as housemaid for a well-to-do family in the Lincombes area of Torquay, South Devon's prime resort for many of the Victorian upper classes.

Florence, a very attractive girl, had everything going for her, but, ironically, that would ultimately be her demise.

Her future was in jeopardy when she found herself trapped in a situation where she was damned if she did and damned if she didn't.

Her family was on the breadline, and given a mean wage, she managed on payday to find a few pennies to give to her mother on the strength that she now had regular board and meals and her very own, sparse that it was, room.

But initially, everything looked good for the eighteen-year-old who could now see her way clear to enlighten herself with the better things of life, and the stable hand, Philip, gave her the confidence of knowing what it was like to be noticed. He was a handsome lad, and, for the first time in her life, she felt the real need for a new kind of relationship other than just friends and acquaintances like former school friends who she still saw occasionally when on some shopping errands for her mistress.

For a while everything went along fine, and she got on well with the other employees like Jean the cook, the two kitchen hands, Ann and Mary, and Joshua, the butler.

She began to strike up a closer bond with Philip who said he loved her, but, although she felt she liked him very much, that was as far as it went. It was her very first romance and, despite Philip's requests, she would not submit to any more than a secret kiss and cuddle when they could both snatch some spare time together, usually in the stables. She argued that he simply could not love her in so short a time that they had known each other, but Philip insisted it was love at first sight.

But in those days for a relationship to progress to any more than that would have been regarded as improper, and Florence was dubious about how her employers would react if she was discovered in a place where she was not instructed to carry out her duties.

One day, she was approached by Mr. Donnel, the master of the house. This had never happened before, and she was concerned that her private visits to see Philip may have been discovered, and she feared the worst, already thinking she must never again visits the stables, even if it meant breaking up with Philip.

"I am having a sort-out in my office and would wish you to help me tomorrow when you have finished your usual house duties," the master stated, and she breathed a sigh of relief that her concerns were unfounded.

"That's very unusual, Florence, "said Jean, "for the master to want someone to help him. Indeed, you had better watch yourself, girl. I have seen the way he looks at you."

But Florence was of an age and a time when innocence was common in one so young, so she didn't take much notice of the head cook's remarks, not imagining for one moment that she would be regarded by a man of such high esteem in being interested in her. And besides, he was married to the mistress, so that confirmed her feelings.

But she was soon to discover his desires upon her, and her innocence was shattered. She struggled with him to stop the things he was doing. He, in turn, was smothering her with compliments, being very aware of her vulnerability and her innocence, telling her that there was nothing wrong in it, that it was the most natural thing in the world and that if she would just relax, he would do her no harm, his intention being to give her pleasure.

"But I don't love you. It would be sinful."

"You silly girl. You don't have to be in love," he quirked. "This must be just between me and you, and no one else must know of it. Then nobody will know you are committing a sin, if that is what you feel it to be. And you will have some coins I feel sure you can make good use with."

"But God will know, sir!"

But such was his lust, he ignored her plea to stop, and all regards for her emotion were abruptly disregarded under the spell of his intent to seduce this very desirable girl, and she was in no doubt that, if she refused him, and that was made abundantly clear, her services would be suspended and she would not receive any reference to find work elsewhere. That she should accordingly think it an honour for a girl of such lowly class to be desired by a man of high esteem, being an important member of the aristocracy.

Later, when she came downstairs to her room, sobbing, she encountered Jean who asked what the matter be. The master had his way with her despite her reluctance, and any notion she formerly held, that that intimacy was linked only within a marriage commitment, was utterly destroyed.

"It is nothing," stressed Florence, "'tis just the time of the month.

"I don't believe that for a moment!" Jean returned. "You are not the first, you know, and you won't be the last. I'll be bound. You look so flushed and beside yourself."

Florence was well aware that Jean knew what had happened, but, of course, she was sworn to secrecy and to be prudent at all times, else she would definitely have to go, that she must be grateful for the master's countenance and be there at his demand.

She clutched the five sovereigns in her hand. He was generous enough but she felt dirty. Her only thought was that it would help her mother get a few things she so desperately needed for the home that they had been living in like slums.

"Next, it will be more, Florence, for I have a lust for you that grows and grows and grows!"

Her master's words and actions flashed repeatedly in her mind as he dressed himself, ordered her to do the same and be off "without so much as a murmur - it is our secret!" he stipulated.

Florence was well and truly stuck between the devil and the deep blue sea, but she couldn't hide her feelings from Jean who was astute enough to know what was going on, and that coupled with a lot of envy. She, having been employed by the family for nigh on ten years, and the master had never given a sparkle for her, was a recipe for resentment which prompted a word in the mistress's ear, when the time was right and the master was taking in his indulgence with Florence once more.

Jean went to the sewing room upstairs where the mistress was busy on the pretense she had a query with the dinner menu.

"Mutton would be fine," the mistress confirmed.

"What about the master, Ma'am?" Jean enquired, knowing the habits of her mistress, that she would go to his study and ask him, for it was not the cooks place so to do.

"Wait there and I will enquire, Jean. Just a moment."

Jean waited with a sly grin on her face and soon, as expected, the mistress returned in a state of hysteria.

"You may go, Jean. We won't be eating tonight!"

A little later, Florence appeared looking very distraught, red faced, and tears streaming down her cheeks.

Of course, Jean didn't really have to ask what the matter was, but she did anyway.

"I don't want to speak about it, but the mistress has dismissed me. I have until tomorrow to pack my things and be off."

"You should have resisted, Florence. Now look at what has happened."

"How could I? He is the master of the house to be obeyed!"

"And I expect, he offered you all the things under the sun, did he?"

Florence looked down and opened her palm and revealed two sovereigns.

"I only hope you don't end up with a bun in the oven."

But Florence was more concerned about her livelihood and what that would incur.

"Maybe, the mistress will forgive me if I explain?"

"Whether she will forgive the master is the thing. When aroused, the mistress is known for her severity."

"What shall I do then, Jean?"

At that moment, Philip came in. It was getting on to dinnertime, and, seeing how Florence was, he went to comfort her, asking her what was wrong.

With her head on Philip's shoulder, she put her fingers to her lips, indicating Jean to hush.

But it was of no use. The next day saw Florence returning to her home not knowing how she would tell her mum. Everything was going so well, and she was happy and contented until the master made his move. She would never ever trust a man again.

Somehow, Philip got word of her misdoings with the master and immediately blamed her, saying that she rebuffed him but let the master have her, he suspecting, it was for his special favours like he would give her money and things, and, being as she was that sort of girl, he didn't want to know her any more.

A few months passed. Somehow Florence managed not to tell her mother what had happened. She did some work locally, casual work to earn her keep and some for her mother.

But is soon became obvious that Florence was pregnant. In those days, a girl was considered to be the lowest of the low if she got herself pregnant before marriage.

Her mother threw her out of the house, despite her daughter having been so considerate in helping her with expenses. In her eyes, she had committed the sin of sins and therefore, in consequence, she was no longer a daughter of theirs.

Florence was on her own now. What should she do? Walking through the village, she saw her former master getting out of his horse drawn carriage and caught his eye.

He paused a moment as if to ask her how she was, but then, seeing her bump, he quickly got back into his carriage.

"Go on then, run - it is yours you know!" she yelled historically, angry that he chose to ignore her.

"Nonsense, girl, we know of your doings in the stables!" and like a flash horse carriage, driver and passenger were gone, and poor Florence left standing there.

An old woman befriended her, and she was able to take refuge until the baby was born in her small cottage.

"Can do it for now, but as soon as you have had the baby, you will understand, you must go because my reputation will be at risk, there not being a man around, you see."

When her baby was born, the old woman helped her, but then said she must leave, and Florence and the baby were out on their own. All she could do was hope that someone would help her. At least she had enough milk to feed her baby, but how long could it last?

The old woman gave Florence an address in Babbacombe, near Torquay where, if there was no possible other way, she could 'farm' out her child, when she could get some cash behind her by working in one of the typical 'workhouses' of the day when women were obliged to work for a mere pittance or take to the streets

But it was late September and getting colder, and she would have to relent, because she could hardly keep herself alive, let alone her four-month-old son.

Charlotte Windsor, a contemptuous woman who ran her business in a large property in Babbacombe and seemingly without empathy or any emotion whatsoever, used the wretched girls, who had got themselves into trouble, to her full advantage, taking in their illegitimate children and babies for a few shillings a week or putting them away for a set fee of £3 to £5.

When Florence conceded that she could not possible keep both herself and her baby alive, she saw Charlotte Windsor who had no conscience at all in offering to 'smother' the child, saying that it was really the best for child and mother, that it would not suffer any more.

But Florence resisted and instead took up Charlotte's offer to take and look after the child from three shillings a week primarily, but when she raised the fee to double, Florence was unable to pay, despite working all hours in the workhouse. She was at her wits end, weak, and trying to recover from a severe mental breakdown and stood by as Charlotte smothered her child and wrapped its naked body in newspaper.

Poor Florence, unable to take any more, threw herself off the Babbacombe cliffs.

The best thing that probably came out of this story, based on truth, is that when the baby was discovered in Babbacombe, wrapped in a copy of the Western Times on the roadside, more facts emerged regarding the ruthless Charlotte Windsor who was later tried and sent to prison for the rest of her natural life, and eventually led to the amendment of the Infant Protection Act in 1897.

The Spirit of Ann Luxon

Taking a short cut through Paignton Parish Church cemetery, I was in a mad rush to accomplish some important research, needing to get to the library where I should have been an hour before. Then, just taking the turn of the path beneath the large yew, making way for the exit gate, I saw her.

I know, it could not have been an imagining, because, for one, my mind was cluttered with what I needed to do, and two, if there was ever any chance of my seeing a spirit, I envisaged a kind of transparent figure with a ghostly, scary presence.

"Cheer up, Peter," was all she said in passing. You know how it is; your mind focussed on anything but where you are, me thinking 'who the devil was that?' She was young, attractive, and she had a radiant smile, and she knew me, but should I know her?

I quickly stopped and glanced around, this in the course of a couple of seconds, so you would think she would still be there, making way for wherever she was going.

But she wasn't. All I saw was what appeared to be a moving cascade of light dissolving into a gravestone.

All thoughts of my project were gone. I just had to step back to the place I had seen the apparition disappear, and, not knowing what to expect, I felt frozen to the spot.

A grave bore the inscription of an Ann Luxon who had died in 1850 aged 20.

I just knew, it was her, the girl who floated past me just a minute before, the girl who wore Victorian garb and the stance of a girl of the period, her hair, her shoes, everything. She had flashed past me, and yet, I remember her like a picture printed in my mind.

Why on earth I should see this joyful young woman, in the middle of the day with the sun shining brightly, who had died so early in her life, baffled me.

Yet, it made me think just how miserable I must have looked that prompted her to tell me to cheer up.

It gave perspective, too, that probably those souls long gone, like Ann Luxon who died so early, can be happy with their lot. But I wanted to know why and how that could be when their tenancy on this beautiful blue planet was so very, very short.

It must have been a week passed when I had almost given up ever seeing the lovely Ann again. Every day I made a point of taking the short cut through the cemetery, pausing to look at Ann's grave, but to no avail, although I noticed on three occasions a black cat passing nearby and, once, perched on Ann's grave. I wondered if the cat had any significance, the way it perched there for quite a long time, not nervous of me at all when I bent to stroke it, then the way it looked up at me, those luminous green eyes. Did Ann have green eyes? I couldn't remember. It all happened so quickly, but I remembered her radiant smile. Now the cat was purring loudly, and when I went to go, it actually followed me, like it wanted me to stay. But being on a tight work schedule, I reluctantly left and hoped maybe I would see it again the next day, like it really had some sort of connection with Ann. Now I was beginning to doubt myself. Was I going nuts or something?

Many folk like to put aside the idea of spirits and the like. Sometimes to talk about it generally may give the distinct impression that you are an eccentric.

I always aimed to keep an open mind, because, maybe there are many things we, as mere humans, do not understand.

When I saw Ann, it was completely out of the blue, but since I saw her I could halt, I could listen and be at the ready to accept any spirit who maybe would like to contact me, but it was all in vain. I came to the conclusion, as the weeks went by, that it is more likely to happen when least expected, so on that count I tried to put Ann out of my mind, although, having said that, I still took the short cut every time I headed for the library.

About a month later, I saw the black cat again strolling along the path where I had seen Ann. It stopped and looked up at me like its eyes were piercing mine, like it was prompting me to stop and stroke it, its head perched up high like its tail. I could not resist bending down again to stroke it.

But then like a flash it had gone, like something had scared it and yet, I heard no noise, no scurry. I looked around behind me again, as I did after seeing Ann. I felt sure, I saw it to dissolve in the vicinity of Ann's grave.

I slowly ventured back, stood by the grave once more. A translucent light shone, and there she was, perched cross, legged on the grave, like a waft of bright mist forming her body, still garbed with the Victorian dress and shoes.

Lost for words, I stood there as if there was a void. I could not say anything. I was utterly spellbound that such a thing could be happening.

Remembering what she had said to me the last time I saw her, I smiled, showed her I was happy to see her again.

"Tommy has a sixth sense like all cats do. He knows you are psychic, and that is why he had led you to me, Peter."

Aghast I asked how she knew my name and, yes, I had delved into the psychic in the past, forgetting it is still part of me, I guessed.

Like she was reading my mind she said: "That is why you can see me, Peter."

Gradually accepting this was really happening, I was intrigued by the charisma and the glow of an aura surrounding Ann, the colours constantly changing from blue red and white again.

An old lady passed by,but Ann said she could not see her, just me standing above. "You may wonder why I am here, Peter."

That had not exactly crossed my mind at that stage. I was more amazed at what I was actually experiencing, seeing a girl who had died so very long ago.

"Do not be perturbed, Peter. There are other souls all around, like me waiting to be sent on but having to settle an outstanding matter relative to their time on earth, so I am not alone."

She smiled beautifully as if to reassure me of her true presence in spirit and soul. She held out a hand, and I felt warmth. A warmth that somehow prompted me to touch hers, but hers had slipped back, and I was touching myself, the palm of my hand laying over the other hand, and I felt a surge of warmth and wellbeing enter my body and quiver my spine.

"To touch thyself is to touch thy soul," Ann whispered so very delicately, and I knew what she was about. She did not have to say anything because we were joined in mind and body.

"Will you find my father? There is something that is imperative he must know before he passes on. He has no need to feel the guilt because of me. His karma tries to do this but he cannot hear. I need you to befriend him, Peter and explain what you already know of me. If he can't hear his Karma, he will never hear me, and that is why I need a living human contact."

Momentarily I was thinking: *Her father?* We are talking over 160 years ago here. Then the reasoning came through…

"Is it that your father had died after you and, as I perceive it to be, Ann, he has been reborn to serve another life here?"

"Yes, you will know that I cannot pass certain knowledge onto you regarding reasons for reincarnation, something known to us and indeed to you when you pass on, but know that the body matter is simply a tool to enable you to manage and adapt in human form on earth."

"And the message, Ann, what do you need me to tell him?"

"It will become apparent to you when you meet him. He is close to hand, and you will know who he is when you meet him

"And what is his name?"

"Henry. Henry Martin. He has lost the Luxton name in the transition."

Although I had no idea what the message was, all seemed to be abundantly clear, and I knew I must find her Father and give him the information in order that Ann can make her long awaited transition, to learn if she, too, must serve another term on earth or go on to something very wonderful beyond the ken of a mere human spirit.

We said our goodbyes. She said, she would see me again, before I took the exit gate. I turned and she was gone, only Tommy, the black cat, remained, watching me as I closed the wrought iron gate behind me.

But was it all some sort of trick of the imagination? Was it just I wanting to believe that I really did see the spirit of this young girl? And, given my writer's imagination, was all that just a figment of that?

I just had to go back to her grave, but now the black cat had gone. No matter how much I tried, I could not see or hear anything. In fact, what I had heard was not in voice form either, as we know it. It was something much more than that, like electricity forming those word variations that had been coming through in a tone, which I believe my mind translated to be the sound of the voice of a young girl.

But if it were real, what I had encountered that afternoon, and how would I know who her father was in this life? I knew his name, so that was a clue. But if I did find the man with that name, what then? He would probably think, I was some sort of freak if I gave him the story translated to me by Ann. But something was about to take place. In life many of us experience things, we are unable to explain but generally shrug off as mere coincidence and be that as it may, but after about six telephone calls from this guy who said he had misdialled when I replied, then tried and tried again, I showed him that I was getting a little cross. But he retaliated, saying that he was certain he had dialled the correct number. I suggested, it must be a line fault and if he didn't mind to give me his number, I would be glad to telephone him back to see what happened.

When I did, he answered: "Henry Martin here. Who is that, please?"

So the first step had been made, and I had inadvertently discovered Henry Martin, but was he the reincarnated father of Ann Luxon, and how was I to find out, and then, if I did, would I be able to convince him?

It seems Henry and I simply could not explain the reason why he kept getting my number when he was phoning a number with the last digit different. My last two digits being 21 when the number he required ended 20 which, thinking about it was Ann's age when she died. But what the significance was, I do not know, but was it possibly a form of electricity given out by her spirit that retracted the digit from a one to a zero?

It seemed complicated afterwards, but at the time it was a simple way of introducing myself to Henry Martin who commented about reading my bits in the local paper and that he would like to discuss a point of issue with me regarding one of my articles about the ghosts of Berry Head Castle in South Devon.

Here was a guy after my own heart, interested in the things that mystified me. We shared a drink in the local pub and got talking. Luck would have it that he had also encountered the ghosts of Berry Pomeroy, and, accordingly, it was easy to gradually enter Ann into the discussion, but could it be that like me, he was able to perceive the presence of a spirit, and if so, why not his own daughter? I perceived that it was probably to do with the fact that he was so close to her.

"So you have seen the spirit of Ann Luxon?" Martin asked, and I explained how it had come about and got onto the subject of what she had said to me, what had come through to me the afternoon I saw her in Paignton Parish Church cemetery.

But there was a certain point when I froze, when I was about to talk to him about the possibility of he being Ann's Father in 1850. Then, of course, I was overstepping the mark. My purpose had been accomplished. Martin was keen to go and have a look at Ann's grave to satisfy his curiosity.

Then it happened, Martin there standing at the grave. But this time I encountered nothing and was beginning to doubt my story. But there was something. I stood back and there was a certain flare of white light that lit up the dull overcast day.

Certainly, Martin was experiencing her presence; that was clear. In a few moments he turned, the white light gone, just he standing there looking happy and very pleased.

"Are you alright, Martin?" I asked

"She has forgiven me, my little girl, who I missed so very much. She is alive and well in another life now, and I will meet her soon."

"You will, Martin?"

"When she died, I blamed myself for negligence, you see, but she made me aware it was not my fault, that the reason she fell out of the coach was not because of the way I spurred the horse on with a sudden jolt, me looking around with horror to see Ann had tumbled out, but on her account as she leant a bit too far over the side to wave to a friend and lost her bearing, just before the horse bolted, it seems."

The sum of all that meant that Martin's conscience was clear, and he had no blame to carry for the fatal demise of his daughter. Now he could live out the rest of his present life and know, when his time came, he would be free of guilt.

Doodlebugs

Chatting recently to a young pal, the subject of war came up, and I suddenly realised the thing about getting old is that all the memories stashed away in those well used brain cells are far from dead and gone. And also you are not on par with those younger generations, simply because they were too young to share those certain memories of way back when. Those which, you would think, would be fairly obvious, really, but I guess at my age one is entitled to have 'senile moments.'

But Bert's remarks querying how it must have been to witness bombs showering down over Britain, saying how he found it hard to visualise, sort of set my brain cells sparking, because I remembered it only too well. All those German bombers hovering overhead, their engines droning with a full load ready to drop over London and the home counties, my family and I huddled in our purpose built Anderson air-raid shelter at the bottom of the garden, just hoping they would not drop their bombs on us.

It is hard to believe now that a family of four, not to mention Tibby, our pet cat, was huddled together in a concrete lined oblong dugout covered with corrugated steel curved strips and overlaid with the dug out earth.

But I was only ten, and it all seemed to be a big adventure, watching Spitfires and Hurricanes engage in dogfights with the enemy above. I remember, too, given all that, how we were always free to ramble the countryside, and if there were an air raid while we were out playing adventure games, we would know the bombers were heading for the built up areas, so no problem.

That was until 1944, when it was a different matter, because Hitler started bombarding us with his new 'secret weapon,' the V1, the first of three 'vengeance' weapons produced in retaliation for our bombing of German cities. The scary thing was, the bombs would crash down indiscriminately, depending when their fuel ran out. Hearing those raucous pulse jet engines suddenly stop was really horrible. We all held our breaths and counted five and thanked God, we were still alive after the culminating explosion.

After that it almost became a daily occurrence, seeing the strange flying objects in the sky at all times of the day. The air raid warning seemed to be forever sounding, but it was not the same as when the German bombers were overhead, because you knew there was no immediate danger until that engine stopped. My pals and I made it a sport to bet when the engine would stop, and if it was anywhere overhead when that happened, we would go scooting for cover. If not then, we would watch it hurtling down and put our fingers into our ears waiting for the ultimate explosion.

69

Once I remember watching an RAF Spitfire from the nearby Northolt base, trying to tip the square shaped wing of one of the Doodlebugs.

We discovered afterwards, the Polish pilot was attempting to make it crash into the country, but, unfortunately, it scored a direct hit on a dwelling nearby, and I remember hearing the resounding explosion.

But before that, in the early summer of 1944, my pal Paddy Green and I, enjoying one of our usual adventurous excursions in the country, amazingly came across one of the pilot-less aircrafts which hadn't exploded, its nose burrowed deep into the side of a hill, not so far from RAF Bentley Priory, the headquarters of Fighter Command during the Second World War.

We had no fear in our hearts, just the spirit of adventure, which, I guess, put all such fears aside. This was one of the first bombs of its sort, so we assumed it was a standard type aircraft because it had wings and a fuselage. We automatically thought it was a plane that had downed and gingerly looked for the pilot. But strangely it had square shaped wings and there was no pilot, no cockpit. We were flabbergasted! And the engine was different, too, no propellers - very bizarre. We scrambled over the fuselage, played sliding games, it was all good fun, that is until we were interrupted by a hoard of civil defence men who piled out of a lorry, which had pulled up in a nearby lane, who were mumbling something about bringing in the bomb disposal squad, then seeing us, looking aghast and yelling to get the hell out of there, that it was an unexploded bomb!

Until then, it had all seemed like a game, and it was being spoilt by grown-ups, but when we saw they were keeping their distance, pleading with us to make a quick run for it, it occurred to us this was serious. What made it worse was when Paddy tumbled after sliding down the fuselage and did something to his leg. I could not leave him there, despite the yells of the defence men. I remember feeling the high tension, and you could hear a pin drop as I attempted to drag him away from the area.

But one of the men came running over and quickly picked up Paddy bodily and ran back to his colleagues where a medic was on hand to tend a nasty wound on Paddy's knee.

In minutes it was surrounded by barriers, which were widely based in a circle around the bomb, and an army bomb disposal unit appeared, scratching their chins and looking truly baffled. But the police arrived, and we were driven home and told not to mention a word to anybody, that it was top secret.

Feeling important and privileged to know something our parents didn't, we held the secret. Well, for a little while that is, but eventually it had to come out. The excitement of it all was just too much to hold back any longer.

My elder brother, George, home on leave from the army, didn't believe us. He thought it was all a game.

"Alright, I will show you!" I doggedly replied, and in a matter of an hour we arrived at the scene on our bicycles.

But there was absolutely no sign of the aircraft. It had gone! Only a small crater remained partly filled in. No way did my brother believe me. It could have been anything. There were no signs of tyre marks indicating maybe a lorry that would have taken it away, just no evidence at all. I felt a complete idiot, and my brother called me a twit, saying I had watched too many adventure movies.

I tried to back my sighting in mentioning, that it was a hot summer, the earth was parched and hard, any evidence could have easily been cleared, swept away. I bought Paddy Green into it, to back me up, but we were a laughing stock, and my brother made a big issue of it.

But later, after the end of the war, I read something that made it abundantly clear. That such an enemy secret weapon, crashing on our soil, would be subject to intense security and examination, I feel sure the nicknamed Doodlebug we saw was one of the first to crash on Britain, and the fact that it was intact, was probably a bonus as far as the experts were concerned. The craft was soon nicknamed the Doodlebug because it buzzed like an Australian insect of the same name. It hurtled through the skies of the southern counties of England at the rate of 100 to 150 a day, and, in consequence, during the first week of that month 2,752 lives were lost and 8,000 injured.

The flying bomb, as we also called it, was fitted with a pulsejet engine with a set amount of fuel to fly it to the given destination, most coming down in London and its suburbs

But it seems to this day, such was the intensity of the security at that time, there is absolutely no record of there having been an unexploded bomb found in Harrow Weald Common. But the memory of my childhood is still strong, and I will always remember the absolute thrill and excitement shared with my pal to this day.

After the war, many facts emerged about Hitler's terror bombs including the Doodlebug and the V2 rocket, which was the baby of all the later space venturing rockets to follow.

Because of my childhood experience, I had a special interest in the making of the Doodlebug, its conception and the reason for using such a devastating terrorizing weapon on innocent civilians.

Although lacking the ability to locate precise target, this new horror weapon was an ingenious invention. Initially known as the Fiesler Fl 103, but more commonly the V-1 (Vergeltungswaffe 1), and later nicknamed the Buzz Bomb or the Doodlebug. It was the mother of all the pulse jet powered type aircraft to follow and predecessor of the cruise missile.

The V-1 was developed at Peenemunde Airfield by the German Luftwaffe, and during the initial development it was known by the codename "Cherry Stone". The first of the so-called Vergeltungswaffe 1 series was designed for terror bombing of London. The V-1 was fired from "ski" launch sites along the French and Dutch coasts. The first V-1 was launched at London on 13 June 1944. At its peak, more than one hundred V-1s a day were fired at southeast England, 9,521 in total, decreasing in number as sites were overrun until October 1944 when the last V-1 site in range of Britain was overrun by Allied forces.

This caused the remaining V-1s to be directed at the port of Antwerp and other targets in Belgium with 2,448 V-1s being launched. The attacks stopped when the last site was overrun on 29 March 1945. In total, the V-1 attacks caused 22,892 casualties (almost entirely civilians).

The British operated an arrangement of defences (including guns and fighter aircraft) to intercept the bombs before they reached their targets as part of Operation Crossbow, and the launch sites and underground V-1 storage depots were targets of strategic bombing.

Although the enemy were unable, with the lack of technical knowledge we have now, to bomb a precise target, it didn't seem to matter to Hitler. With the threat of invasion becoming imminent, he strived to break the morale of the British in a last ditch effort to turn the tide by scaring the populace at large. But, nevertheless, it wasn't for the want of trying.

A specially modified manned version of the V1 was built with the mission to create a system that could direct the craft, if not to a precise target but a specific known area, which would cause the most damage to the allied war effort. And a lot of energy was put into that objective in determining how much fuel would be needed for that purpose.

And it was by no means smooth going. In an effort to adjust the V1's settings regarding the guidance system, German intelligence needed to know where the bombs were landing. German agents in Britain were requested to obtain this information, but it seemed the agents, aware of the way the war was going, changed sides or became double agents and nothing could be verified or confirmed.

Some of the bombs had been fitted with radio transmitters but, initially, they were not at all competent and were responsible for many short falls. But when they actually did get correct readings, Max Wachtel, commander of the FLAK Regiment was not convinced and was inclined to go for the agents' evidence. Having compared them with the findings of those agents, gross discrepancies occurred. The commando, believing the error was because of their transmitters, went for the evidence obtained from the agents.

It has been said, if Wachtel had disregarded the agents' reports and relied on the radio data, causalities might have increased by fifty percent or more.

Although initially the V bombs were built in the mode of war and caused much havoc, the experience gained through the demands of war created the know-how to progress to new and improved technology of which the German's are famed for.

But always and forever, I shall remember the sound of those raucous engines and then suddenly, the scary silence, waiting for the inevitable explosion.

"Fete" Accompli

Now, young Dillon was not aggressive by nature. But when in front of everybody, when he deliberately toppled Julia's stall, some may have thought otherwise.

It was so very much out of character for Dillon to behave this way. Whatever had come over him?

Without a word of warning he just appeared and placed his hands under the stall and whoops! Absolutely everything went tumbling all over the grass, and Julia was at her wits end, attempting to salvage undamaged items, lifting up the folding table and replacing the wrecked cup cakes with a fresh supply from a closed tin box underneath the stall.

It was the time of the annual Cullington village fete. The venue was in the large vicarage garden overlooked by the Anglo Saxon church of St. Mary.

The day before, poor Julia Timothy, the chairperson of the Women's Institute, slipped from a chair whilst putting up bunting. Dillon said he had fixed the chair, too.

Never mind, today she could relax behind her stall and watch the world go by. That was the plan, but Dillon had other ideas.

It was no joke. The look on the lad's face was enough. He was angry, angry with Julia.

The reverend Auberon Beasley, sampling one of Julia's apple and cream delights at the time, the remnants of which were now plastered all over his charcoal grey suit, was angry too.

"Now, Dillon, that's no way to treat your mother," the reverend resounded trying in vain to clean down his suit with a sponge given to him by a lady at the next stall.

"She's not my mother; she adopted me," Dillon declared, his eyes glued on Julia. "I have just found this letter which proves it."

He waved a piece of paper above his head.

"You lied to me. I really thought you were my mum!"

Everybody heard Dillon shouting, they couldn't help but hear – and the way he was behaving, too – disgraceful was heard to be said by several onlookers. Friends and colleagues congregated nearby titling and tattling. Julia had always played so much on how she nearly died when Dillon was born. Auberon Beasley was lost for words.

Dillon turned to face the man in the dog collar, snarling and pointing an accusative finger directly at him, his long brown hair hiding much of his face: "And you needn't look so shocked. I know you are my dad. You a Christian man, too. You must have broken at least three commandments!"

Now silence reigned; that last remark did it - no titling and no tattling. Auberon froze for a moment but managed to put on a nervous smile, prompting everybody to look around the stalls, telling them to enjoy the day, promising everything would eventually be explained.

He grabbed Dillon's arm and firmly led him away in the direction of the vicarage, calming him, telling him they must talk, and giving the shell-shocked Julia a nodding wink as he did so.

As the children did their dancing bit on the green to the accompaniment of a small one- man disco, small groups of folk were still talking about the scandal. But when they passed Julia's rebuilt stall, they respected her embarrassment and said not a word.

But one could hear old Jack Bellinger's voice ranting on, showing no consideration whatsoever for Julia. He was the village builder, stood outside the beer tent, punctuating his words with swigs of beer, a rough and ready 'take me as you see me' character who said what he thought, no matter what.

"What do you think of our vicar then?" he asked the woman next to him, his voice slurring, his mouth twisting. "What a scandal and he being a confirmed bachelor, too. I wonder who the real mother is. Some local girl, I'll be bound."

"I don't think it is any business whatsoever of ours, Jack Bellinger," the woman scorned. "And you should shut your trap!"

"That's telling him!" mumbled someone nearby.

Aubrietia Jay, serving light refreshments, heard Jack's comment. She pondered whilst pouring tea into lines of cups set upon a tray. The cups overflowed and so did the shallow plastic tray, the hot liquid made like a stream for the table edge. There was a deafening scream when Henrietta Berkeley, clad only in a very revealing low cut mini dress, screamed she had been scalded, although there seemed to be no evidence of this. The on-site first aid nurse attended after breaking through a host of lads offering their assistance, Henrietta lapping it up and loving the attention. Another girl serving nearby, who obviously didn't like Henrietta one iota, commented she was there and saw what happened and no way did any of the hot drink splash her, she reckoned her aim was to get out of the chores, as well as being fussed by the boys.

Then Aubrietia, unaware of Henrietta's dilemma, ran over to Jack Bellinger and thumped him on the chest yelling: "What bloody business is it of yours?"

Tears flooded her face. She was not interested in Jack's reply apparently, just wanted to get it off her chest because she immediately returned to her stall, collected her handbag and made for the ladies room.

"Why! It's 'er, innit? It's gotta be," Jack grunted, insinuating Aubrietia must be the mother, "else why would she say that? Come to think of it, she's always running around the vicar. I've seen her many a time sidling up to him when I was repairing the church steeple, like she was a demented teenager looking for her first date, always there, always around since she came into the village, pandering to 'im. And he be a rogue, the vicar too, wonder what 'er husband will make of it? Doesn't' say much for 'er either, she who professes to be unblemished and perfect. Huh! You can tell 'er sort, all prim and proper on top but underneath ..."

"Jack," interrupted his wife Joanne firmly, with an even more bellowing voice than her husband, firmly talking him down. "You are only assuming. Things aren't always what they appear to be."

Bert Jones the church warden, who had been ear wigging, was sceptical, however. "I don't know about that, perhaps I shouldn't say this… Well, I wouldn't at all if all this hadn't come up… But even vicars are human. If Aubrietia took his fancy, who are we to make judgment? We don't know the underlying current after all. But now it's a different matter. As a Christian he must act accordingly and come to terms with Aubrietia."

Everybody agreed. They were ready to set up a petition to spur their vicar onto the right course. They were a close village community with strong feelings.

Ken Everett, the local newspaper reporter wanted a quiet word with Bert: "Are you sure about the vicar and Aubrietia... I mean have you actually caught them, well you know...?"

"Well. Not exactly but when she's doing organ practice, and I have seen his arm around the woman. Who knows what they get up to later?"

"The mind boggles," Ken grinned mischievously, thinking it could make a perfect scandal for the Sunday's if spiced up a bit. He needed more facts. What about young Dillon, how did he know the vicar was his dad?

This was the biggest scandal that had hit the village since Councillor George Biggerton was caught out in 1968 using the mansion house for the use of private orgies for his friends and associates. They never saw hide or hare of him after that, he quickly moved incognito to a place unknown after

76

he had been sentenced to eighteen months imprisonment for inappropriate use of council expenses.

Later that afternoon, it was prize draw time. Auberon was designated to present the prizes. He coolly appeared showing no sign of embarrassment. The absence of young Dillon was carefully noted. Auberon approached Julia and spoke. Those watching noted carefully reactions and expressions, anything that was likely to muster a clue of what was going on. The way she looked at him and he at her. Was there any sign whatsoever of the lust bug or the glint of love?

"Are you alright, Julia?" enquired Joanne Bellinger who was quickly on the spot just as soon as Auberon had departed, itching to find out the score.

"Yes, I've sold nearly all my goodies, thank you, Joanne."

"Yes, yes, I can see that. What I mean is, your Dillon, he looked a little upset. Is he alright?" Joanne asked carefully.

"He is now, just a mix up with the timing, that's all. And I think he overreacted a bit. Auberon thought he had gone too far. You know how difficult teenagers can be these days."

Joanna did not quite understand what Julie meant but assumed she was making light of it. What a brave woman. Reluctantly, the subject was dropped. Perhaps she would tackle Auberon. By coincidence he called her name at the moment of decision. Looking up, she saw him holding a large box of chocolates.

"This is for you, Joanne. Ticket number thirty-four. It's got your name on it." She took the chocolates without even as much as a thank you, snarling up at him. How could he just pretend like that, when everybody now knew about his sins? She would catch up with him later. She would make sure of that.

Auberon gave a resounding thank you to everybody who attended and contributed. The man on the keyboard played his last number, and the stall participants started to pack up.

Some waited expectantly for Joanne who was seen chatting with Auberon, Dillon and then the newspaper reporter, Ken Everett, to see if they could gather any more information about what had happened and what it was really all about.

Everett descended first, armed with notebook and pen and looking very pleased. He muttered something to Bert about it not making the Sunday's but it would be good for a laugh in the local rag.

Then his attention was caught by a group of laughing teenagers carrying video equipment and cameras followed by Julia and Dillon, laughing and chatting. All was well, it seemed. Dillon acknowledged the stragglers outside and it was to be seen that, strangely, no more animosity was shown by Dillon towards Julia

"Thanks for your wonderful performance," Dillon praised, "without which we couldn't have got the atmosphere. It was fait accompli or should I say fete accompli?"

Last out was Joanne, accompanied by the vicar. She looked sheepish and embarrassed. She spoke very precisely to the waiting group.

"It seems the village drama group are making a film about social problems. It was all an act. I just want to make it crystal clear that all that has taken place between out embellished vicar, Dillon, and Julia was pure fiction. Cameras were set up on the vestry roof to film the whole thing. There were even couples amongst the crowd. They wanted realism. The only way they could get it was to keep it all quiet. All our reactions, everything has been recorded."

Auberon was the next to speak. "I do hope it will not cause too much embarrassment. It was a very good opportunity for our young people to make a film, which I hope may prove useful. If you want to know more, come to the church on Sunday. My sermon will be about the wrongs and rights of judging others, how we should obtain the facts before making conclusions. And, of course, all those who appear in the film will need to give their consent which, given the circumstances, that all proceeds will go towards the upkeep of our deteriorating church roof, all will agree."

"About Aubrietia... Was she in on it, too?" asked Joanne.

"Well, no," Auberon smiled "It's just that she wanted to protect her brother from any false accusations."

"Her brother?"

"Yes, sorry. Didn't you know? I'm Aubrietias brother!"

If it Hadn't Been For You - A True Story

As a fully trained RAF medic I was posted in 1952 to the RAF Hospital Halton in Buckinghamshire, England.

I was put onto the medical and surgical wards for a while but was transferred to the Tuberculosis unit, which was built on a high ridge of the Chiltern Hills.

It was all new to me but I felt well placed and felt I could cope with the trauma given to those poor guys who had invariably picked up the infectious disease after coming into the service.

Because I had a good positive resistance to the disease and under the strict service regulations, I was able to work on TB wards for a period of not more than six months.

I was to learn a lot about human courage, weakness, and myself in those months and also those 'angels,' those special people who worked alongside with me, the doctors, nurses, and the general medical staff who gave so much of themselves in pure devotion to their work.

An imperative part of the treatment for TB patients was the intake of the clean, fresh air. During daylight hours, even in the cold depths of winter, patients were moved outside with their beds onto the wide veranda adjoining the ward. The colder the air, the better the treatment, but they were well wrapped in an abundance of blankets. Bed warmers were a must.

A half bottle of Guinness was another important and very welcome part of the treatment, which could last for weeks on end. It was certainly a morale booster for those poor guys who suffered the torment and boredom of days in bed with, perhaps, according to the severity of their illness, a stroll along the ward and some browsing in the well-equipped library.

No TV in the wards then to ease the boredom.

One poor guy in my care, I shall call Des, grew deeply depressed. We got talking. I soon realised that conversation was an important factor, but, as a medic and to do your job properly, you needed to keep your distance. That for me was one of the hardest things I had to achieve, because I was brought up with the caring and consideration syndrome of my parents.

One of the most difficult tasks I had to accept as a medic was to remove from his bed a patient called Tom who had just died, whom I had spent much time trying to beat him at chess when I had a spare moment.

He had suffered the horrendous trauma of having a large cavity eat away his left lung, and for those medics like me, who knew him and tended him, we felt sheer relief that Tom would suffer no more. But just to touch his lifeless body was something I could not bring myself to do, just to help another medic remove him onto a trolley for despatch to the morgue seemed an impossible task when my body seemed completely to freeze.

Going through my mind, he had only been talking to me an hour ago and now…

For that brief moment, I felt all my aspirations in my medical career were wrecked. However, could I be a true medic if I could not handle this?

But the staff-nursing sister came to my rescue as if from the woodwork, just a push in the right direction, and I was there, my hand touching the legs of the guy who had passed on.

Tom's passing had a serious effect on Des whose bed was next to his and with whom he had befriended. I remember his expression after we had drawn back the curtains surrounding Tom's bed, seeing an empty mattress and no more Tom. He was crying like a baby, but when I tried to comfort him, he disappeared beneath his bed covers. The senior nurse prompted me just to leave him, which was probably the best thing.

But all this did have a derogative effect on Des. He was no longer sharing hopeful thoughts with me when we spoke. He told me, he had lost all hope, that he felt he was absolutely useless and convinced himself that it was just a matter of time before he would be joining Tom.

I reminded him about his girl in whom he had everything to live for.

Des always kept a photograph of his fiancé on his bedside locker. He confided to me, he was the luckiest guy in the world to have a girl like Linda, but she didn't deserve this, for him to be tucked away in a hospital bed for weeks on end, when she could only visit once a week because of the distance from home and what she was able to afford.

A big factor, too, was that in being confined to bed for so long did nothing for natural progression, especially if you were so much in love. It is true that many of the patients in my ward became frustrated and frisky, and the intention to cool their ardour was a daily measure of bromide. In those days, in the early fifties, to talk sex was still taboo as many still held the belief that sex before marriage was sacrilege! And yet, being sexually frustrated was considered to be a definite setback for cure when a mere shadow on the lung became a spot, then a cavity, and I was sad to have lost three patients in a fortnight that winter.

I could see a definite improvement when Linda had visited, and there was the smile on his face again.

80

As a special favour, Des asked if I could draw the curtains around his bed when Linda was visiting. And why not? It may have been scorned upon by the senior nurse, but I was able to convince him that Linda could probably do better for Des than any known drug.

"But, Pete, you and I know, any intercourse would do more harm than good in his condition."

"You have much to learn about how it is between couples who are deeply in love, Colin. He and she will know the boundaries, and the last thing Linda would want is to harm him."

"So?" Colin questioned as if to prove his point.

"There are other ways," I added

I will always remember Colin's response, just the look that said everything, first the confused frown and then the look of knowing, then the smile and the little nod that followed. I had no need to say more and the curtains remained drawn.

But Linda's visits grew less. Des would not say why, but I had a feeling it was his doing, since he had changed after Tom's demise

After a spot of leave and returning to work in ward TBH 1, my first port of call was Des, because his bed was the first in a line of twenty, there being ten each side all taken.

Seeing Des looking so glum, I asked him if he was all right. He said nothing but just turned his head to his bedside locker. It dawned on me that the picture of Linda had gone.

"We have broken up," he said very solemnly. "It's just not fair on Linda. She's a lovely girl, and she deserves only the best. Look at me. I am as good as crippled with a hole in my lung. What good will I ever be to her?"

I remembered seeing her on a couple of her visits. She was certainly a lovely girl with a heart-warming personality. Des had introduced me to her as the guy who keeps him under control. They looked so happy together. As if by fate, I just happened to notice the remains of Linda's photograph torn to pieces in his wastebasket.

He was breaking the news to Linda by way of a letter, which he asked me to drop in the post box for him. I was loath to do that. If only I could have encouraged him to change his mind. Many patients, just as severe as Des, recovered to live near normal lives. But, despite my efforts to convince him otherwise, that he must fight for the sake of Linda and his family, he had the idea in his head that he was a goner. If I was going to be absolutely honest with him, I could not give him false hopes. There was great concern for Desmond, but while there was still life there was hope.

In the morning I distributed the morning streptomycin jabs. In those days it was the wonder cure for Tuberculosis given a strict regime of cool fresh air, and we were grateful for that. But sometimes the drug was limited when the hole was severe and had actually developed into a cavity.

The distribution of codeine pain relievers was then commonplace, too, and Ethambutol played a big part.

Often and unofficially, we gave out placebos we called sugar tablets to ease the pain many suffered, some more than others, depending on their pain level. It was amazing how they worked, patients believing they had taken the real thing and, of course, the benefit was fewer side effects that some standard pain relieving drugs would cause.

Of course, I had to post the letter. But not without noting the address, so I could follow on with one of my own. Perhaps, I was stepping out of line, but I just had to speak with Linda.

She telephoned me the next day, beside herself with deep emotion, telling me just how much she loved Des, that it didn't matter one iota about his condition. She felt sure, they could work it out together, that she needed to be close to him, especially now. But that could not be, and he was adamant about that. He never wanted to see her again, and she just couldn't understand why. Did he not know that true love means accepting each other no matter what?

I told her what I knew. That he really did love her. There was no other reason why he was breaking with her other than what he imagined to be his own shortcomings.

"I simply must see him again. I just can't go on like this," she cried.

"It will be okay, just you wait and see. Give it a day or two. I'm sure he will come back to you." I was being positive.

I would try, carefully and gently to persuade Des that there indeed was hope and just to talk about it with Linda, that she loved him that much, she did not want it all to end like that. But Desmond was a hard nut to crack.

Unfortunately, my hopes were in vain. I had spoken with him briefly on just two occasions before he was sent to Midhurst TB Hospital in Surrey for further specialist treatment.

Life had to carry on; there were other patients in the ward just as unwell as Des. Linda never contacted me again. Months passed, and for me it was the end of the story. I dared to hope, it was a happy one.

Twenty years later I had a letter from a source in Bristol. All it said was for me to meet this person outside the railway station there on a given time and date.

I searched the depths of my mind, wondering whom I knew in Bristol. Then it came. Des, he came from Bristol. Could it possibly be him, had he fully recovered?

It was. There to greet me was Des, Linda, and their two teenage sons. They really just wanted to thank me for my perseverance and involvement back at Halton. Des said, they had been searching for me for years. They finally caught up with me when they saw an article I had written in a railway magazine. It was to do with the rail crash at Harrow and Wealdstone in 1951. He knew, it was the same Peter Carroll because there, perched on top of one of the broken carriages, helping with the rescue work, was a picture of me. I had told him about it, too.

But they wanted to surprise me, and that is why they apologised for not signing the letter asking to meet me.

It was a great, great moment. One I shall never forget.

"If it hadn't been for you…," Linda smiled.

That said it all.

Pio Grech

In August 1952, my first posting out of medical school as a fully trained Royal Air Force Nursing attendant was to Princess Alexandra's RAF hospital Halton in Buckinghamshire, England.

The hospital was well equipped with the latest technology of the time, and I was to become well versed in the wonder of plastic surgery.

On my arrival at surgical ward I was met by senior nursing sister, Shirley Hubble, about twenty-five years old, I guessed. She had a pleasing warm smile, a blonde with blue eyes, and she was very efficient and positive in her approach.

"I have got a special for you, Carroll," she advised. "His name is Pio Grech, and he arrived last night, flown over from Malta by air ambulance.

"A real sad case he is, Pio. He is a Maltese from Valletta, and he is a civilian who was working under the jurisdiction of a British service contract.

"Employed as a driver, he was transporting canisters of sulphuric acid on a flatbed loader truck when he crashed and overturned on a steep hill, fracturing one of the canisters which, literally, poured over him from head to toe. You'll specialise during the day, we need to keep constant watch."

Reading the notes, I saw this case was going to be a challenge. Sister Hubble directed me to the screened area in the main surgical ward and pulled back the curtains.

"Good morning, Pio," she announced brightly. "I'm introducing you to nurse Peter."

I winced when I saw Pio. I was astounded he was still alive as Sister Hubble removed and replaced each dressing. He had horrendous burns. Must of the extremities were absent or severely damaged. Pio had also been blinded in the accident, his eyes severely damaged, the outer covering of flesh burnt away.

I caught Sister Hubble's glance, which said everything. I knew I would have my work cut out, and Pio would need my complete care and attention.

Pio responded with a slight head movement and an attempted smile. What was left of the flesh and muscle surrounding his mouth was taught and raw but he was able to issue a sound and move his tongue.

"Fortunately, Pio speaks English quite well," Sister advised. "His hearing is fairly good despite having lost his ear lobes, but you will have to speak up.

"Because the skin nerve fibres were burnt he suffers little pain, he has some feeling in his fingertips though. You will need to change his dressings twice a day. He is constantly losing body fluid, and you will see he is on a saline and plasma drip."

Sister gave me the notes with an optimistic smile.

"He's all yours, Carroll. I know you can cope," she encouraged. "Doctor Richer will be doing the rounds this morning. Apparently they sent him out to Malta to pick up Pio. He specialises in burns, and it's his first day at Halton, too, so you will have something in common."

I drew up a chair to the bedside and made myself comfortable. I had to get to know my patient, to reassure him that he was in good hands. Dedicated to my work, I was determined to give it my all, and being thrown into the deep end as it were, I knew I had a task as well as a challenge, and aimed to face up to it.

"Okay Pio?"

I saw Pio's blinded eyes flicker as he responded to me with a delicate movement of the tongue. I was able to understand that. I could just make out he was asking how I was.

"I'm okay, Pio. How are you feeling?"

Over the next few days I was able to quickly adjust to the treatment and needs of my patient. It soon became evident that Pio was aware of the extremity of his injuries, but did not crave for or want pity. Doctor Richer said it was a miracle that he was still alive, and he must be blessed with a tough resilience and willpower.

One of my regular daily jobs was to pull out with a pair of delicate tweezers the dead nerves, which looked like strings of black cotton on his bare flesh. He could feel nothing of course and took it all in his stride. The courage and humour of the man were absolutely beyond belief given his injuries.

He was an example to all, and I have never known anything quite so humbling since.

Other patients in the ward had also suffered horrendous injuries, but none could match the intensity of Pio's.

They found comfort and hope in his dogged humour and spirit. He was soon the most popular patient in the ward, and the other patients admired and respected him. They teased him about hogging the female night nurse all to himself- who like me had to constantly be at his bedside - but he took it all in good heart.

In the next couple of weeks Pio's condition worsened. He was still losing body fluid, and the saline and plasma drips were stepped up. Due to the inability to move his lower jaw Pio was on a feeder tube. The whole ward was a quieter place now. We feared the worst.

The hospital psychologist felt certain Pio's extraordinary mental resources would pull him through, but he needed something to spur him on.

The plastic surgeon, Wing Commander Shuttleworth, and the eye specialist were ready to start work on Pio. With a skin loss of eighty per cent there were limitations on how far to go. If Pio gained strength, the eye corneas could be replaced.

The answer came in the post the following morning. Pio's brother was flying over from his home in Sicily. I could see the joy on Pio's face when I told him. He wanted to shake hands with me but his was too fragile, and he had only two movable fingers on his right hand. I interlocked them with my own right index fingers.

"Let's shake on it," I laughed.

It was to become our own method of greeting. We called each other 'Muckers,' the lingo then for good mates.

The news about his brother's forthcoming visit acted like a tonic and immediately he was back to his old self, full of that Pio fighting spirit we all admired so very much.

Then he told me something. He told me his parents were killed during the heavy war bombing on Malta. During the war years the small island was used as a garrison for British troops and earned the honour of the George Cross

Then he said, "I do have a girlfriend in Valletta, Peter." He had never told me before. He seemed now to want me to know.

"By now she will have forgotten me and found another. I don't care. I am not attainable for the present."

We both knew what that meant and I knew that, on the premise he would survive, would be a future problem to overcome.

Joe arrived a couple of days after, simply not believing the awesome figure on the bed was his brother. Before I could let him anywhere near Pio, he had to recover from the tears of horror. I said he could take tea in the ward office until he was ready. He had to be brave for his brother.

He showed me a recent photograph of Pio, a very handsome dark haired lad of eighteen. It was hard to picture him now being the same person. But it helped. Pio's face now showed no trace of character - nothing. I made

86

an automatic imprint of the photograph in my mind and would remember it always when I spoke to Pio.

"Pio, your brother is here to see you."

As I spoke I watched Pio's joyful reaction. His whole face quivered with excitement, and he lifted both bandaged arms to greet his brother. This was a time to take a back seat and leave them together.

"I'll be in the ward office if you need me, Joe," I advised.

Joe opted to stay for a few weeks. He was anxious to do all he could for his brother. Pio had very little healthy skin left on his body, and Joe offered to give some of his.

Thin strips of skin were carefully sliced from his thighs and grafted to Pio's body. The surgical team had to be sure that any underlying damaged tissue was restored before any implant could successfully be achieved.

Pio took on the appearance of a Tailor's dummy covered in papier-mâché, but he was always brave and cheerful about it, as if he was blessed with an invisible force.

I never believed in guardian angels until then, but certainly someone was watching over him in a way no human could.

Joe was brave, too, if only for his brother. But he had many reservations about the future. The Doctors were unable to give any firm assurance. Pio could never be the same again. He could never be a whole man, he would possibly be blind for the rest of his life if their planned corneal transplants failed to take, and the extent of the damage caused to his muscular system would undoubtedly restrict mobility.

The strain began to take its toll on Joe. He became a nervous wreck, sometimes finding it difficult to control his emotions, even in front of his brother. I was a good listener, but my reassurance had to be limited.

"What future is there for him, Peter?" he asked the question knowing the answer and continued.

"He will be an old man before his time. I have a wife and children to think about. I have to put them first, you understand. I have to return to them. I could never put them through the trauma of seeing Pio."

Joe was crying now. Out of Pio's earshot, he collapsed into a chair in the ward office and sunk his head onto his hands. He was shaking and pleading with me.

"What can I do, Peter, what can I do?"

I knew there was nothing more he could do. The tension and strain had worn him down. He was close to a nervous breakdown. He was having a battle with his conscience, and he wanted to find a way out to avoid the guilt of having to leave Pio.

The next two days were, for me, leave days. I travelled down line to my home in Harrow Weald and relaxed in the garden, my once pride and joy before joining the services.

When I retuned, Joe had gone. He had returned to his family in Sicily.

I didn't know what to expect when I returned to the ward and Pio. I was concerned his brother's absence would cause an emotional set back. When I greeted him the usual response was there but somewhat deflated. Uncharacteristically, Pio sat upright in his bed and said nothing. His ward colleagues seemed to know his pain, and instead of the usual verbal friendly banter a polite word or two was exchanged. I decided just not to say anything about his brother. Pio had all worked out all right, and he knew the score, how his brother just had to return to his family. Within a week, he was the same Pio again and everybody breathed a sigh of relief. What courage and understanding this young man sustained has remained with me all my life.

But no one is indispensable. Next month I had a new posting to an RAF hospital in Rostrup in Germany. I had trained up a new specialising nurse Michael to take over, and I shall never forget that last week at Halton, how Pio and I shared the special memories we already had in just nine months of knowing each other. Those cherished discussions about our beliefs and so forth. Pio was a spirit unto his own. He was surely blessed with a wonderful guardian angel.

After my posting I tried to keep in touch with Pio but that was difficult.

Later in the same year, whilst on home leave from Germany, I was able to visit him at Halton. He was still blind which told me the cornea transplants had not been successful. But the highlight of my visit was when I approached Pio who was seated in his chair next to his bed. It had been eight months since last I saw him. I said nothing at first but watched his expression when I performed our special handshake and yelled: "Muckers!"

He knew me instantly, and that really meant so much to me. And still does, even as I write.

He was eventually sent home, I was told, but that was the last I ever heard of him.

I would not be surprised if he pulled through; he was that sort of guy. I prefer to put my faith in God who, bearing in mind his awful injuries, would ascertain which fate was the best for brave Pio Grech.

Second Chance

I was in my element. This was what I had craved for. I had never passed anything first time and having achieved just that, I was flying my second solo flight in a husky bull-nosed North American Harvard/Ar-6 trainer.

I had made a good job of the first solo, landed perfectly and did all the things I was supposed to without a hitch.

In the early fifties there was a shortage of the RAF standard type air training Provost airplane, so I had the privilege of flying one of the newly delivered Harvards as used for training purposes with the Royal Canadian Air Force and loaned to the RAF as a stop-gap until a new batch of Provost jet trainers arrived.

I felt this was my baby, and I was on top of the world, maybe just a little overconfident feeling like I was a veteran pilot, and I could teach those stuffy flight instructors a thing or two. I guess, I wanted to show off to Jonny, the instructor who accompanied me in another Harvard alongside, just in case I needed help, and having done a couple of loop-the-loops to the reception of a hearty "Bravo!" from Jonny I was brimming in confidence.

Then something went wrong that I couldn't explain.

"Get those bloody flaps back up, you're not landing yet!" I heard Jonny yell through my headset.

Now I was confused, and, suddenly, all my confidence was gone when I realised I could not move a limb, no way could I adjust the flaps or do anything else. I suddenly felt useless and vulnerable and so wished my instructor was there, back in the cockpit behind me, to put things to rights.

I heard the frantic yells coming from Jonny, telling me to up the flaps and level flight but it was too late. I was already in a spinning dive. It was all like a dream, it just didn't feel real - all that training, the hard swatting, it felt like it was just a figment of my imagination because this just couldn't be happening to me, the ground whirling nearer and nearer to me, everything to the side-vision blurred and disfigured, then blackness, nothing, like I was a goner, a little too much too soon, Jonny should have known I wasn't ready. But, why - why did I freeze? And why blame Jonny? I remembered part of a Shakespeare line from Julius Caesar.

"The fault, dear Brutus, is not in the stars but ourselves"

I shall never know to this day why, and yet, just maybe someone up there knows, and it was for a purpose.

I discovered later I was in a deep, deep, long coma. I distinctly remember that tunnel with the brilliant light at the end I have heard so much about since, that others have experienced, that so-called 'near death' experience. Primarily, I was gutted that I had messed something I wanted so very much, remembering as an eleven year old, watching the RAF Spitfires from nearby Northolt aerodrome battling overhead with the German Messerschmitts, and just how I was wishing it was me doing all those tricks to avert each other's fire, the rolls, the sharp turns, looping the loops and the victory roll when one of them scored a hit.

But now I was completely alone in a void as it were, feeling no pain, no real sensation, and it all seemed so tranquil. I felt at peace, no stress now, no pressure about doing the right thing and getting it right. For a moment, I knew not how long because time seemed not to be the essence, time didn't matter anymore, like it was an earthly thing to guide us during our tenancy there. Was I any longer part of it or was this it? That light at the end of the tunnel shining through like a beacon, as if drawing me closers to the other side. Was it a sort of consciousness or was it a dream? Was it real or was I done for? Maybe this was a passage through to - I know not where, because I never reached it, and I guess if I had I would not be telling this story, anyway.

I needed to go back from whence I came. Please, please, I am not ready to die, not yet, please, Lord, give me a second chance.

Nothing! Or was it nothing? Perhaps a whisper, just a sound hardly heard but whatever it was, I just knew I was not ready for that other place and the tunnel was bending in on itself, squeezing me out. The choir stopped, and I heard a soft gushing noise, like the sound of a gushing stream.

I felt completely unable to move a muscle or speak, even as though I distinctly heard muffled voices. Had I returned or was this another place? There was darkness, but I remember how I wanted to open my eyes to see light, how I wanted to talk to communicate with someone out there.

It seemed a terribly long time before I heard more voices, still very muffled like they were distant and barely audible, higher sounds of females and the lower of males.

"This patient, I do believe, won't make it. He has been in coma for how long, Sister?"

"Six weeks, Doctor, but I feel there is something there."

"Sister, there is nothing. I have tried all the tests. In my opinion, we had better let the poor bloke have some peace and let him move on. We cannot just continue to keep him alive on drips and oxygen, there is absolutely no sign of brain activity, nothing!"

I was thinking, they couldn't be talking about me, must be another patient then.

"He was lucky not to have been burnt alive when the plane exploded on impact."

"Was he that lucky though, Richard? He'd apparently been catapulted out of the cockpit as the wing of his aircraft hit a tree just before impact, and thrown into a recently ploughed field. It is amazing, but only his head was fractured. Is he that lucky? And would we be wise to keep trying to bring him back, how would the brain damage affect him? He has lost a good part of his brain."

I was going through the motions of trying to respond in some way now, knowing they were talking about me. Do they not realise that I can hear them? Everything they say! If I could just make some sport of sound, move my lips, my hands, my fingers, anything. I just had no control over my body whatsoever, but I dearly wanted life, it was so very precious, but was I destined to go back into the tunnel.

The female voice was obviously the nursing sister the way she was talking, how I had at least responded well to a major operation in repairing my skull. She was saying something about I had responded, so there had to be hope, and I just wanted to grab and hug her, in my mind saying, please, please, help me through.

Then silence again, it lasted for what seemed a lifetime and having absolutely no control of my limbs or anything I wanted and hoped they would not give up on me.

But the silence prolonged, and I was beginning to think all hope was gone. It was like I was falling, falling deeply into a sound sleep, or was it the long sleep that I would never wake from.

***

"Peter?"

It was like my eyes were stinging. I was looking though an incessant waterfall trying desperately to focus on a face behind.

"Peter, thank heaven, you have proved me right. I knew you would make it!"

I felt myself smiling with utter relief that at last there was someone out there realising I wasn't a goner and still very much alive. I tried to talk but somehow couldn't get the words together.

"No need to talk yet, but you shall be able to soon. Just pleased you are back with us, Peter. My name is Sister Susan. Okay? I will be specialising you until you are fully recovered. We need to do it together, you and me, huh?"

I nodded, realising at least now I could do that. I could move my lips, too, and make some sort of sound. I could even wiggle my toes, and I heard Sister Susan chuckle. "We shall soon have you back to normal, Peter!"

In the next few days I had my station RAF commanding officer come to see me, joking with me over what a way to prang, but I knew they would want to do an official inquiry, but that would come later. I was assured by the CO not to worry. I was alive, and that was the main thing.

Then, as I felt more with it, some of my other colleagues from the base were able to come and see me two at a time as rules and visiting hours were very strict in those days.

I could see they both felt sorry for me and happy, too, that it was a miracle I had survive at all.

I just had to accept my lot. No way would I fly again, even if I would be allowed to. There was the question of fitness, but I always had it in my veins that I would have loved to have tried, to prove to myself that I could do it.

I told Sister Susan, I loved her for having so much faith in me that I would pull through. She smiled beautifully, saying how many times she had heard that before when assisting a post-operative patient who has been classified as a serious case.

For a while, though, I felt I really did love her. "I would have thought you would have had a girlfriend out there," she enquired,

"My love is flying," I replied wistfully immediately, realising after I had said it that was positively a no-go.

It was as if she read my mind because then she said: "Well, now you may be able to concentrate on what else you will do with your life, and maybe soon you meet a nice girl."

Of course, I would get nowhere with Susan. She was just doing her job, and I came to realise that she was just a very nice person who was in my life for those brief weeks, like ships passing in the night, but for me she helped restore confidence in myself once more, knowing that, maybe, I would be left with the aftermath of what my injuries may incur.

When eventually I was released and having trained firstly as a medic in the RAF, I was well aware of the concerns regarding how the loss of part of my brain may affect me. It is remarkable how much we have progressed in fifty years and how little was known about the functions of the brain.

It wasn't long before I had to return to hospital for a brief spell because of severe headaches. It was then they discovered that because my head had been badly fractured, and they had to make up a plate to tuck in beneath my scalp, to cover a cavity about the size of an old penny - the volume of cerebral spinal fluid I needed was less because of the dent in my head, but the body was still producing the same amount as before - thus the severe headaches. So, in order to decrease the pressure, I needed to regularly undergo a lumber puncture which eventually cleared the headaches give a year or two, and the amount of fluid my body produced was in synch.

But the RAF, needing to try to assess why I had frozen and lost control of my aircraft, and, also eager to learn how the brain loss may affect my mental ability, had me visit their psychiatrist on a monthly basis when I felt like the proverbial guinea pig given numerous mental ability tests with a host of electrodes attached to my head and chest.

And two years later when I met Daphne, I was still occasionally having headaches and once or twice suffering a loss of consciousness. Once when we were out together, I imagined I would be a hopeless partner in marriage, which we both wanted.

"I may not even be able to have children with you," I told her sadly, but she seemed adamant she wanted me anyway, and I guess this is what secured our love for over fifty-two years. And now we have two grown-up sons and four grandchildren.

The best thing about my near death experience was that it made me really appreciate just how privileged we are to enjoy a comparatively short tenancy on this wonderful blue planet, and it has given me a faith in my Karma that has seen me through thick and thin.

For Freedom

The night was calm and tranquil, but the stones and rubble left from the Second World War made the Lincolnshire scene unreal. The weather had changed, and droplets of rain covered the windscreen.

James, my nephew, suggested we ought to call it a day. We had set out early to take in the old airfield trail of North Kesteven in Lincolnshire, England, to take a look at some of the former World War Two Royal Air Force bomber and fighter bases as described in a very useful booklet published by the North Kesteven District Council, but dusk was early because of the overcast sky.

Many of the runways and support buildings had become ramshackle giving off an eerie ambience. In my mind I could almost see aircrafts taking off and returning from the business of war, those returning being the fortunate ones.

Then I saw it, coming in low, an old wartime Lancaster bomber. Flames were gushing from one of its four engines, and only one of its undercarriage wheels was visible. It seemed to be heading directly for us.

My mind flashed, and there was a bright white light which dissolved, and it was like I was there, in that bomber, being part of the crew and just having been hit by a German fighter at about 20,000 feet after our bombs had been dropped successfully, and we were climbing out of the target area. The captain had taken evading action at once, but the enemy secured many hits. A fire started near a petrol tank on the upper surface of the starboard wing between the fuselage and the inner engine.

Davy, the Australian pilot, was yelling: "We've been hit! Starboard engine on fire! Any ideas?"

Then I saw Norman, a fire extinguisher in his hand, and, shuffling near to the pilot, he quickly jettisoned the escape hatch above the pilot's head and clambered through.

"What the hell are you doing, Sergeant?" Davy yelled, but the noise of the engines almost drowned Norman's reply as he pushed his head down through the hatch and said he could deal with the problem, but asking for the Captain's permission. But then he was gone again, and I just couldn't' believe it when I saw through a starboard window what he was about, clambering along the wing he made for the flaming engine. It was madness. It would mean him holding on with one hand and using the other to operate the extinguisher.

Davy struggled to hold the Lancaster level as he and Tom, the navigator, watched with disbelief as Norman directed the extinguisher into the flaming engine.

But Norman's mission was impossible. The force of the rushing air swivelled him around on the wing face like an autumn leaf falling to the ground. Tom was attempting to grab hold of his gear, yelling at him in an attempt to get through the noise of the engines "to get the hell back here," but it was to no avail. Poor Norman was a goner, dropping aimlessly into the darkness below, his flying gear in flames, his hands stretching upwards into the air as if he was still clutching into the edge of the wing.

"He's a goner, alright!" yelled Tom. "What courage! Hope he is gonna be okay. He has a parachute. Can't see if it opened though. Too much cloud."

"At least the cloud is keeping the searchlights off us," commented Davy. "We don't want another hit right now!"

But then all seemed lost as the engine exploded, but the fire went out, so perhaps the wing was still intact, and Norman had done his stuff. It was quite possible to fly on three engines so long as they remained stable and, even though Davy had doubts about the damaged undercarriage, they headed home rather than ditch in enemy territory. But another engine was beginning to splutter and spark. Would it hold until they reached base?

My mind flashed again, and I was back standing on the runway, but I could still see, as plain as I could see James at the wheel of our car, the low flying crippled Lancaster coming closer and closer.

Beforehand, I had persuaded James just to drive us to Metheringham before we made for home.

"Let's just see the disused airfield," I urged. The booklet said that many of the Lancasters used in the bombing of Berlin were based there. It was particularly interesting, because much of the old runway and perimeter track was still intact and used as a road to Blankney Fen.

"To drive along this old runway would really be something," I said. "And there's a memorial up there to the left."

I had read that 106 squadron flew over two hundred missions over a period of twenty-two months from Metheringham and suffered fifty-seven losses, aircraft and men who failed to return, most of them losing their lives. A few, the lucky ones who managed to bail out, survived as prisoners of war.

James had lost some of his enthusiasm, I thought, but I had to realise, he was only twenty-five. How could he have been so keen as I, who remembered how those days were? Had I been just eight years older I could have been flying those old Lancasters. That was in 1943. But ironically, I could have been killed, and maybe in one of those fifty-seven doomed bombers, the price both sides had to pay for war. Instead, there I was in 1998, attempting to picture the scene during those hectic war years.

We had driven about a half mile when I asked James to stop. I just had to tread on the old concrete runway, thinking about those poor souls who never returned. To think they were so young, even younger than my companion, but such sacrifice was deemed necessary by "Bomber" Harris who wanted revenge on the German bombing of our large cities.

When I was a kid, the RAF pilots and aircrew were my heroes. Brought up in North London where the blitz was horrific, I had experienced the horror of the German bombing and was fortunate to survive.

Looking up, I realised the overcast sky had broken. The full moon was low, partly shrouded in black ribbons of cloud known as a 'bomber's moon.' One could almost feel the vibration of those many Lancaster bombers. It was so loud, loaded with bombs and on full throttle at take-off to gain those first vital feet. I stood where hundreds of bomber crews had passed over.

Yet at that moment there was silence, utter silence, like there was an angel passing over. I felt it appropriate in paying homage to all those lost who took off from that very runway on which I stood. It was bizarre. I felt I was hearing whispers of voices in the light evening breeze, maybe remnants of those chattering aircrews hyped up for yet another mission and the possibility of not returning to their loved ones. How brave were they, knowing and trusting the pilot was able to weave in and out of the flak of the always severe ground fire. It would take only one hit to do the business. Many of those who did return, filled with absolute gutted sadness, had seen their mates literally blow up in their flaming craft or floating aimlessly to the ground.

So much responsibility had been put on the young flyers of 106 Sqn. Harris used them to the full to bring down the morale of Nazi Germany. At the same time, we all thought it was right to fight the good fight, to get rid of the Hun. They had really tortured us with aimless bombing. Now it was our turn to put the boot in.

A little further up the mile-long runway we saw, adjacent to the runway, the memorial to 106 squadron. James pulled up again for me to have a closer look. It was then that I heard the sound of droning engines like the sounds remembered from my childhood. I turned to see the flaming bomber descending. It was a wartime Lancaster bomber all right. What the devil was it doing up there in 1998? As I watched it coming closer, I suddenly realised that our car, with James at the wheel, was smack in the middle of the runway, right in its path. I yelled at James, who seemed unaware of what was happening. He just sat there reading a map, and didn't hear me. It was going to be too late. The blazing aircraft was almost at touchdown.

There was nothing I could do. I watched helplessly as the bomber hurtled towards James. Its one undercarriage leg collapsed, and suddenly there was an agonising crash, and the sound of scraping metal was horrific. The whole mass spun and shot off the runway, just missing our car. James was still reading his map. I just could not believe it. I closed my eyes and shielded my head, waiting for the imminent explosion.

But nothing!

I looked up again. Everything was as before. James came over to me. "You alright, Pete?"

It was something that had happened in my mind; that was all. Or was it? I had the idea that perhaps it was one of the missing aircraft of 1943, caught in a vacuum of time and still trying to make it back to base.

I assured James that everything was all right, and I looked at the memorial again. I felt very humble because I was there, using their runway. The runway itself is also a perfect memorial to a great squadron well known in the annals of the Second World War. Perhaps, it was all in the mind. Now, there was just peace. I guess most of the crews were tied up in the business of war, as if there was no time for fear. The souls of those who never returned were freed, except for just one bomber crew who were destined to return in a crippled aircraft which, I feel, would have exploded on landing. Are they still up there, attempting to make a safe return? I would like to think not.

When I left Metheringham, I felt no need to return again.

The motto of 106 Sqn was "For Freedom." Farewell, 106. For freedom you fought well.

***

RAF Metheringham was a Royal Air Force station situated between the villages of Metheringham and Martin and 12.1 mi (19.5 km) south east of the county town Lincoln, Lincolnshire, England.

Operated as a bomber airfield during World War II the station opened in October 1943 and was decommissioned in the spring of 1946.

Although now mostly returned to agricultural and commercial uses the site retains one original runway, the eastern perimeter track and some contemporary buildings together with a No. 106 Squadron RAF memorial garden and a visitor centre.

And there are still signs of the once active airfield, many of the original buildings still remain, and the former ration store has been restored and now houses a great collection of photographs and memorabilia recalling life and times on an operation Second World War airfield.

But the most amazing thing of all was the story of Sergeant Norman Jackson, a flight engineer of a 106 Squadron Lancaster who, during a raid on Schweinfurt from Metheringham during the night of 26 -27 April 1944, did go out on the wing of the aircraft in mid-flight and extinguished an engine fire caused by a German fighter attack.

Although he lost his hold and appeared to be plunging aimlessly to the ground, his chute opened and, despite being burned and landing heavily, he was captured and spent the rest of the war in captivity.

Sergeant Jackson was awarded the esteemed Victoria Cross for his selfless act of extreme bravery in attempting to save his crew.

Hollywood Harrow Weald

During the late forties I was absolutely mad about movies. The idea of making a movie myself with the help of my young pals in our street was my ambition. Television was generally unheard of as were, of course, computers. Kids made their own entertainment in the comparatively empty streets when cars were afforded generally only by the well-to-do, and most provisions and consumer goods were delivered by horse and cart.

Youngsters occupied themselves quite happily playing marbles, conkers, hide-and-seek, hop- scotch and many more games. But I had other ideas and, being encouraged by my parents that I was a real natural entertainer at heart, we set up a ramshackle stage in the back garden and started a local talent show, which was a real hit. It soon became a regular highlight and, always with the help of my musician dad who played piano to accompany the shows, we had plenty of youngsters wanting to show off their talents. They loved to dress up and don themselves with false moustaches, beards and the like, and the girls scrounged old hats and even wigs from their mums, and soon, even the adults were coming to see the shows.

I just loved the slap-stick and it is a wonder I survived not suffering any serious injuries given the nature of my mad-crazy performances, the jumping, the juggling, and the twisting as I made a right clown myself, but the kids and the adults who attended loved it, and their laughter and applause meant so much to me.

I wanted to go on to making movies. I had a lot of plots for storylines to involve the best of the pick of the local kids who wanted to act.

It was a regular thing for youngsters to attend the 'Saturday Morning Pictures' at the local Odeon cinema and for the sum of sixpence we would enjoy the antics of Roy Rogers and his white stallion called Trigger, his memorable westerns, co-starring his wife, Dale Evans. Another great favourite were 'The Dead-End Kids' later called the 'Bowery Boys with Huntz Hall.' And during the interval, we all joined in watching the moving ball on the screen, showing the words to popular songs of the time, which we sang along to.

I was always conscious of the kids who could not afford a ticket. So often I let them in through the side inner opening door. It was a wonder, I was never caught, but looking back, I have a feeling that probably the manager knew about it, but chose turn Nelson's blind eye to some of those who had suffered the loss of their dad and loved ones in the war.

Watching those films, I felt I wanted to join them, to be part of the wonderful scenes projected on the screen, but I knew that was only a dream. But, never the less, in 1947 my elder brother, who was serving in the army at the time, presented me a 'gun camera' used in the war by RAF pilots to record 'hits' in shooting down enemy aircraft. The camera was cleverly housed alongside the gun holding on the right wing. It would shoot automatically in sequence with the firing of an aircrafts' guns. The idea was to record hits on enemy aircraft. It was bulky and the recorded pictures were poor in quality.

But for me it was the start of something I so much wanted to do and so 'Cinecarr Film Productions' was born in my hometown, Harrow Weald. We used my bedroom as an office and our address became The Hampden film studios in Hampden Road, and the thrill and excitement of being filmed was magic. And soon afterwards I was presented with, as a birthday present, a new Bolex 16mm clockwork film camera, which regularly required winding up when shooting, and that really set the ball rolling. Cinecarr films were really in business filming our very first movie.

Cinematography for amateurs had not reached its peak and made for an expensive hobby in those bleak post-war days. But without TV to distract, homemade entertainment was very much the in thing.

I had started work at Kodak, joined the works photographic society and was able to purchase cine film for a third of its retail price.

So our first feature film was started. The local kids were anxious to take part. My younger brother John, his pals John Hurley and John Day actively took part in production, casting and acting. Being the initiator, I proudly took charge of scripts, direction, and cinematography.

Exterior locations included our local town, Harrow Weald, near the bus garage, an old barn on Harrow Weald common and, of course, Hampden Road. Traffic was not a problem, only the well-off could afford cars, and many scenes were enacted in the streets. On completion the films were 'premiered' on a large screen made from an old white sheet in the back garden, with the projector housed behind the window of the first-floor bedroom.

The youngsters sat on homemade benches, waiting excitedly to see themselves on screen. They had to wait for the dark evenings of autumn to see the films outside, and the chill in the air did not stop the youngsters from coming.

Having usually about an hour to fill before it was dark enough to project the films, local talent filed the spot. Some performed a dance routine.

Others recited their own poems, and, of course, there were the inevitable singers who often times got booed. But it was all in good fun, and I made sure that, if any of the performers got upset, he would get those who booed to try and do better themselves or apologise.

It made for a great evening of entertainment. My family assisted with music, and they had contrived all manner of objects and contraptions behind the screen to provide sound effects for the silent films.

I read numerous books on 'how to' and started cutting and editing endless feet of cine film, removing erroneous scenes and rejoining the film with amalacetate film cement after having completed the laborious task of scraping off the film emulsion so that the cement would seal satisfactorily.

Mum often came in to bring me refreshments to find me surrounded with cut clips of film hanging on wooden rails and erupted in laughter, seeing me scratching my head in trying to find a particular cutting to join in sequence.

Looking back, I had the most wonderfully patient parents who gave me every assistance in the making of the movies and sometimes even taking cameo roles when we needed an adult in a script.

One of the main problems was incurred in the waiting a fortnight for the films to be processed, when on return we eagerly examined the shots, hoping they had come out how we wanted, but often we had to go out on a particular location to re-shoot a scene, which somehow went wrong or was under- or over-exposed. I was still learning the art and was once almost at my wits end, having to spend more money and time on a shot, which still wasn't right after three retakes! But I was given fresh hope when I read a book explaining that even the professionals often have to do numerous retakes.

But my pals were always eager, and so it was easy to direct them to act my film story how I intended. But looking back, I was really horrid with them if they didn't get it right the first take, and I was partially eager to get the scene completed before, say, a heavy shower stopped filming. But they seemed to put up with me regardless, I guess because of the sheer thrill and excitement of seeing themselves on celluloid and maybe, too, they felt like real film stars when often hoards of people surrounded us when doing a take, making us feel very important. It was all great fun and when we had finished one film, I had another to follow with titles like: *Boy Detective, Two Bouncing Cubs, Johnny's Birthday Dream*, and *Tibby's Revenge*. Sometimes I just opted to find suitable locations at random, if I saw something in my travels when riding around on my bicycle. I would make a note, without even thinking of asking permission of anyone who may have owned the site, yet we were never approached or thrown off. It seems everyone was taken up with the magic of film making and treated us like veritable stars.

We had lots of laughs when things went wrong and sometimes delays when one of the leading stars went down with an illness, which was common in those days, remembering how I lost two brothers with pneumonia. Fortunately none of our stars died, otherwise we would have been in dire straits.

For *Johnny's Birthday Dream* I needed to shoot a dream sequence, which meant a double exposure. I had no special feature on my camera, so I figured a way to do it manually. The important thing was never to let the light get to the unexposed film. I worked out the timing on a sequence after the first shot was completed, buried myself deep under the blankets of my bed, making sure there was no light coming in at all. Then I opened the camera casing where the film spool was lodged. I rewound it with steady fingers to the point where I had started the film earlier. Gasping for air, I succeeded, and the double take was successful first time, which led to more special effects of which many amazed me how I did them.

The exterior film shows continued, There was a great silent film library in nearby Cranford, and I wouldn't think anything of riding the five miles and back to hire out a couple of films for the shows. There were plenty to choose from like the always-popular Charlie Chaplin movies, Laurel and Hardy, of course, and Harold Lloyd, and the inimitable Buster Keaton. The library was stacked with cans of movies, which was always a delight to look through, and they boosted the showing of my own films.

However, there is always likely to be a complainant where there are lots of youngsters making a racket, and one night a policeman appeared. He just stood there, not a word was spoken, and his expression said it all. He seemed almost as excited as the kids watching those films. He complimented us in giving the youngsters something special in their early lives. The only problem, he said, was that someone suggested we were making a profit by taking an entrance fee of three pennies in which case we would need a license. However, when my dad showed him the takings set against costs of hiring our movies and the making of our films, the takings were much less, so happily the show went on.

Later I tried my hand with the documentary films, some in colour, and made a film of the Kenton ATC Squadron band playing at an air show to commemorate the battle of Britain. Disaster struck, and a Mosquito crashed into the car park killing many. It was all very frightening, and I had just filmed the aircraft and the bulging black cloud of smoke rising slowly in the summer air. But the show carried on, and I admired the pilots. They were so brave.

They didn't have much money in those days, rationing was still in force, and food and materials were sparse.

Youngsters were still dying of diphtheria, pneumonia and TB, but the trauma of being killed in a war was over, and we made the best of it.

Unfortunately, Cinecarr Productions was short-lived. I was called up for National Service, and that was the end of it. The world was changing quickly, and amateur silent movies lost their magic. It was the end of another era, remembered with great affection.

Julia and Paul

Linda didn't like Julia. She was the new girl in the office, having been transferred from another branch of Rickley and Mayer, Electrical supplies Ltd. But it was nothing to do about the fact that she had been instantly promoted to head accounts clerk. It was since she had seen the post card in her desk. How could she be so heartless?

She told the other girls in accounts: "You won't believe this, but Julia's intended has lost his hand when working away on a building contract. But oddly, she has said nothing." Linda, being of a very inquisitive disposition, was frustrated.

"So how did you know?" asked Janine. "If she hasn't said anything, how you could know? You have been snooping, I bet!"

The other girls just looked, and their expressions said everything. They were angry. Linda was always snooping about looking into other people's private things.

"One day, she will go too far," Gillian barked after she had noticed on more than one occasion her drawers were slightly open when she returned from lunch break, and she was always most particular in closing and locking her drawers. She assumed, Linda was the guilty party.

Janine, too, had noticed on several occasions that her things had been disarranged in her drawers, saying that, for instance, she always kept her pen and pencils in her right drawer, but after a search there they were inside the left one.

Was it the boss who was fumbling around and, if so, what was he after? But it did give cause for concern that, even although nothing was missing, the thought of someone looking through your things was a bit scary.

They didn't want to make assumptions without evidence, but it did seem more likely that Linda was the culprit, her being just Linda. She never seemed to get the message when, on numerous occasions, she was going on about someone or rather, making all sorts of accusations about the boss was having an affair and suchlike, and the girls just getting on with their work, ignoring her. But she still nattered on.

They secretly hoped that, if the boss got a sounding of her accusations, she might just be given the push for ferocious slander, unless she was right, that is, and the boss really was having an affair, but then who with? All the girls were looking at each other, but there was Angela in deliveries and it was noted - by Linda, of course - that he was often away for an hour or two at a time, heading in that direction.

"Hey, look at us," Janine announced. "If we don't watch out, we shall be thinking like Linda. She is having an effect on us!"

"Yes, let's just stop it, shall we," put in Gillian. "And, anyway, if the boss is having an affair, it is entirely his business and hoping his wife doesn't find out. Although, I must admit, Richard is rather nice!"

"Gillian!"

"What, Janine?"

"Stop it!"

And she did, both of them exchanging a knowing chuckle.

But the girls were interested nevertheless in what Linda had to say regarding Julia and her intended. The couple were an item, so what Linda said did raise some concern as to Julia's true feelings for the guy.

They were to be married in the autumn, just three months away. Now the doubts if Julia really even cared for Paul. Losing a hand was serious stuff, yet Julia was so cool. As if laughing and giggling wasn't enough. Why no tears for Paul?

"Perhaps, that is her way of holding back the tears. If so, she is very brave. Imagine, how it would feel losing a hand, especially if it was your right hand and if you were right-handed," said Gillian.

"Hey, look," said Linda. "See who is going off with Richard. Wonder where they are going?"

The other girls looked confused.

Julia? Could it be Julia having an affair with the boss? Linda piped in that she has seen her go off with him on several occasions. But where? And also there was the business of her just in from another branch, having been instantly promoted. And how did she achieve that then?

"It is all most probably quite innocent, and Richard is simply showing her the ropes of how the set up works here in the various departments. That's all."

"Showing her the ropes I bet!" Gillian quipped.

"Gillian!"

"I know, I know, Janine, we should think pure thoughts, but there is no fun then!"

"Shush!" Janine whispered. "You know how Linda is. She may just take all this seriously and then we will all be in trouble. So shut it! Huh?"

But Linda couldn't hold herself back any longer. After she had returned with the boss, she asked Julia about her guy in a rather probing manner.

"Last heard, he'd got the sack, your Paul," Linda said trying to keep cool.

"Well, that's Paul for you," sniped Julia in return. "It's all his own doing. It had to happen. He was forewarned, was he not?"

Linda was having difficulty in not giving Julie a piece of her mind. There was Paul, minus a hand and sacked into the bargain. She didn't love her guy. How could she?

Responding to Linda's frown, Julia coolly said it was no problem. "Paul drives a large van now, and he's happier doing that. He always wanted a driving job."

Linda was stuck for words. How could Julie be so absolutely callous? If she had a gorgeous boyfriend like that, she would be very concerned and most probably in tears, let alone being able to come in to work.

She quietly relayed the news to the other girls during the morning break. Julia was a smoker, so she was out of the way outside.

"This is really weird stuff," griped Linda. "Not only couldn't Julia care less about Paul, but he's driving, would you believe."

Ann, who was the supervisor from the processing department and who regularly joined them for break time, advised that, no way could Paul be driving after recently losing a hand.

"What about the insurance and everything? Not to mention his ability to drive. Apart from that he would still be recovering after an accident like that!"

Now everyone in the office began to have doubts about Julia. Was she on the level, or was it all make-believe? Was there really a Paul, and was she really to be married?

"I have seen his picture, and so have you. You can't miss it, it is on her desk plain as can be," Linda interrupted.

It was all becoming too confusing and no matter what the reasoning, none could come up with a realistic solution.

Linda said, she would find out just what was going on. She just had to know the score. As much as the other girls resented her snooping, she had their full support for once.

She approached Julia angrily after break time.

"Just happened to notice the card Paul sent you, while he was working away," she said.

"Working away?" Julia snorted. "He was only a mile or two down the road."

"But I thought…" queried Linda. "Well, the postcard?"

Julia giggled. "Oh! That's just Paul. It is all part of his façade. You'll see him later. I know that's what you want."

Linda glanced at Paul's photograph on Julia's desk. She wouldn't mind. He was a bit of a hulk. But Julia interrupted her thoughts.

"Hands off. He's mine. He's picking me up from work, see."

Linda pressed on. She wasn't going to stop now. "Hope, he will soon recover. Is he well enough to pick you up?"

Julia looked puzzled for a moment, but then her expression changed.

"You mean the bug, Linda. How did you know? Yes, he will be here. Wouldn't miss it. Tonight we're going bowling with Jason and Liz."

All the office staff listened intently. They were as confused as Linda whose tone of voice now sharpened. "How can Paul play bowls with just one hand?"

Julia looked blankly at Linda for a while, and then instinctively turned to face the other girls in the office. In a while thinking about it, she caught on.

"It's the postcard, isn't it?" she asked out loud. "The one in that came yesterday's postbag. Look, here's another. It arrived this morning."

She fumbled in her bag and brought it out, handing it to Linda. "Show this to the madding crowd. You really are the most!"

When Linda read the message on the card her reaction was slow. Julia grabbed it back again saying she would read it out for all and sundry to hear. She did just that.

"Better luck today, darling. I got two hands back. Card playing is great when you've got the knack!"

Martin Bolenski's War

June 18, 1944, high above the streets of North London: Martin Bolenski manoeuvred his Spitfire and zoomed up behind a flying bomb, one of the first of Hitler's secret weapons with which he hoped to finally break the dominant spirit of those who had already and so defiantly withstood everything the Luftwaffe had dropped on them. Sgt. Pilot Bolenski's guns were aimed carefully at the craft's right wing. Its engine could stop at any moment sending it hurtling downwards. Martin needed choosing the right moment; shoot now and the bomb would crash on the town below. He had to wait until the pilot-less aircraft reached over the open grasslands of Harrow Weald common. No danger there.

Early in 1944 the V1 flying bomb, nicknamed the Doodlebug, began to drone through the skies of the southern counties of England at the rate of 100 to 150 per day. In consequence, during the first week of that month 2752 lives were lost and 8000 injured. Many of the bombs were downed over the ocean by allied fighters, but, because of the numbers, many filtered through to reach their destinations, with just enough fuel in their tanks to reach London and the suburbs. The first Doodlebug fell on London in Chiswick on June 13th 1944

When Hitler's blitzkrieg crushed Poland in 1939, Martin's parents and his younger brother were killed instantly during an air raid over Warsaw. He was the lone survivor. Intent on revenge, he fled to England and joined the RAF. He trained to be a pilot, something he wanted more than anything else. He lacked the academic qualifications required to gain a commission, but it was of no consequence because the RAF were desperately short of pilots and took on non-commissioned personnel to fill the required numbers. He joined the ranks and achieved his ambition as a sergeant pilot in 1943, claiming to be the proudest Pole in the unit when he proudly displayed his wings sewn onto his uniform.

Martin was accustomed to aerial combat by this time, having covered several sorties and in the space of ten months, achieved several hits on manned enemy aircraft.

Like other surviving pilots he was an expert on the art of manoeuvre in defense and attack. But this was his first sortie involving the new peculiar unmanned aircraft. They were sitting ducks for the enthused young airmen, but attack and destruction was a completely different ball game. Ideally, it was better to destroy them in flight, but this proved to be difficult and at least a couple of Martin's Squadron had bought it, flying headlong into the resulting explosion. The idea was to go for the starboard wing, put it into a spin over the country where the bomb could do least harm. This was Martin's intention; miss the wing and hit the fuselage and he could have been no more, and there was still the possibility of bullets ricocheting. It was no mean task.

But Martin's plan was doomed. He adjusted his speed to chase the V1 as he sighted the open space of Harrow Weald common about a mile ahead, weaving his Spitfire through the column of black grey exhaust smoke billowing out from his target. When the smoke suddenly stopped billowing out, he knew the fuel was spent, the craft with its lethal load started to lose height dramatically. Martin spotted parkland below to his left. In one last desperate effort he fired at the starboard wing, his intention to tip the target enough to create a slow sideways descent, just enough to cause it to crash into the open park. For a moment, losing sight of the V1 as it plunged before him, he put his Spitfire into a deep dive. But suddenly, horrifically, it loomed barely ahead of him, as if motionless. He twisted the Spitfire steeply starboard, but it was too late. His right wing spliced the doodlebug's tail rudder in half, sending it hurtling straight down. As he circled, he was stunned as he saw the bomb hit a row of houses.

Martin was grounded for six months. He managed to guide his crippled Spitfire back to base but twisted on landing. The plane lurched upside down onto the perimeter fence, and he survived with a fracture to both arms.

"You are safe, Bolly. You could have died! It was horrible. I saw the wreckage after they pulled you out. They said as you pronged, your body was thrown from the cockpit onto the wire perimeter fence, and you bounced back into the marsh there. You were very lucky indeed, darling."

Martin smiled, looking up from his hospital bed, relieved and happy to see the smiling face of the beautiful girl who agreed to be his wife. June worked in the NAFFI services canteen at the Northolt base. That is where they had met a year before. His command of the English language was good, but sometimes, when he spoke quickly, the words were unclear. This is how he earned the nickname 'Bolly.' June had mistakenly thought his Christian name was Bolenski. "I'll call you Bolly," she chuckled and it stuck.

June cupped his face in her hands, bending to him, her clear blue eyes scanning the dark wavy hair and bushy moustache of the guy she loved. "Poor Bolly," she said looking at his plastered arms. "Is it painful, darling?"

He looked into her eyes softly and brushed the tip of her nose with his. "It's fine, don't worry."

He was still smiling as he touched her lips softly with his own. Then he started to chuckle.

"Bolly!" Her voice was harder now. "I know you are happy to see me but when kissing - it is not the time to chuckle." She had picked up on some of the idiosyncrasies in his broken English. "Why do you chuckle that way?" she asked inquisitively.

"If I said 'Bresty' you would know?" he grinned. She saw the mischief in his eyes and realised what he meant.

"Why, Martin Bolenski, I ought to ... look, the ward sister is coming. I told you, we don't carry on like that in England. Whatever you Poles say is one thing, but we are a lot more reserved here."

"Polish, English, even treble Dutch, we all love the same way, June darling"

"Double Dutch," June interrupted with an academic smile.

"Okay, double Dutch. It means the same, June. I love you!"

"And I love you, Bolly."

"And I love you, Bresty." He kissed her warmly. It was their little secret.

In a week Martin was discharged but still with both arms in plaster. The CO gave him some extra leave, and it would be weeks before he could fly again. June welcomed the opportunity to pamper him and help him with the chores. She scrounged a few days off to be with him.

Martin billeted in a holiday chalet near his base, one of a number the RAF requisitioned during the war to house the large number of aircrew there.

They spent time walking. Martin loved the English countryside. He was able to gather his thoughts now, having been tied up for so many months in the business of fighting the enemy. They talked of his childhood in Warsaw and the sad death of his family.

Sometimes they took a flask of coffee and a picnic, spending whole afternoons in the country, watching the coming and going of fighters above.

But it wasn't long before Martin became frustrated. He had come to England to fight the cause, to avenge his family, to rid the skies of the enemy. June tried to come to terms with that, tried all the ways to make him just relax, that soon enough he would be up there again, and she would be on tenterhooks, hoping every time he would return.

But just being with June was not easy. He wanted to make love all the time, but with two plastered arms it was sometimes impossible. They found ways to overcome the problem, but he felt awkward and limited. Sometimes they both culminated in roars of laughter. He just wanted to love her without limitations. June was always reassuring, he had to be patient, and soon he would be rid of the plasters and be strong again.

When June returned to work, and Martin was rid of the plasters, he still had a couple more days to run on his leave, and he took the opportunity to drive to Kentley. He wanted to see the extent of damage caused by the doodlebug he had encountered. He felt terribly guilty about that, but was reassured by his station commander that he could have done nothing more, given the circumstances.

He gulped when he saw that three houses had been levelled to the ground.

"Bloody mess, ain't it?" Martin hadn't seen the figure of a uniformed middle-aged man come up behind. He saw he was in the home guard and greeted him with a careful smile.

"Hmm, Pole, aye," the man grunted, sighting the polish insignia on Martin's uniform. "Bloody RAF did this. Our own people shot down the doodlebug right into those places. Six of the occupants were killed instantly. If the bastard had left the bloody thing alone, it may have landed out of harm's way."

"Or killed someone else elsewhere, who can tell," returned Martin.

"Not one of you Poles that shot it down, was it by any chance?"

It took just one punch from Martin to down the man in a moment of fury, all that pent up frustration coming out. He didn't like the guy's attitude. He told him so as he lay there, sprawled on the ground, rubbing his chin. A girl in her early twenties came running to the spot and helped the man to his feet.

"What are you doing?" she screamed. "This is my Dad. Leave him a bloody alone."

She was hammering into Martin's chest for all she was worth. "He's just lost Mum in that inferno over there. He just doesn't need this. Just sod off and leave us alone!"

The girl cried bitterly. Martin managed to eventually calm her, and she found comfort in the arms of her father.

"I'm sorry. Look, I came here, because I wanted to apologise, okay? It was me who caused this. I tried to avert it, I really did. Please believe me." Martin, too, was nearly in tears. The atrocity of war had caught up with all of them. But in the midst of their anger, a strange calm emerged, and they were suddenly void of reason, entwined in the arms of each other.

Martin spent the rest of the afternoon in the temporary home of the father and daughter, which was filled with the items they were able to salvage from the debris of their former home.

They shared tea and conversation, introducing each other: Molly, and her dad called Tim, and Martin Bolenski. They had something in common to share. They had all lost loved ones in air raids. As far as Molly and Tim were concerned, there was nothing to forgive. Hitler was the true cause of the deaths in their families.

In the next few days, Martin found himself unwittingly drawn to Molly. He discovered her hopes and dreams, and it seemed quite natural when a genuine loving relationship followed without reservation. Martin knew he had to tell June but found difficulty in doing so. He loathed hurting her, the girl who loved and cared for him, and he was so very fond of her. He thought he loved her, but since meeting Molly he knew what real love was.

He was soon back to A1, and the Medical Officer gave him the go-ahead to fly again.

For a moment, his romantic problems merged into the background. He was doing what he wanted to do. Fight the enemy, the only way he knew how, behind the guns of a brand new Spitfire, given more height and manoeuvrability

The Squadron Commander instructed the crews on their next mission. The Squadron was to escort Lancaster bombers for a large raid on an ammunition dump. Martin had been the victim of some humorous remarks from his flying colleagues. He had scored ten hits on enemy fighters without even as much as a scratch, yet it took a pilot-less aircraft to make him bite the dust.

"All the best, chaps," encouraged the Squadron Commander. "Find yourself a Jerry, and chop his tail off, but not with your wings!" The crew looked at Martin and laughed, and he took the banter in good part. Well, he would, wouldn't he? He was back in the war and ready to go.

But this time he failed to return. Was he going to be one of the high percentages of wartime pilots who never returned?

"I think Sergeant Bolenski's really bought it this time," the squadron leader reported on their return. "He nose-dived into drink, engine ablaze!"

But Martin had somehow survived. He had managed to cling to the broken wing of his Spitfire and was picked up by a Dutch fishing trawler.

"You will have to hide in the fish hold," the captain advised. "We are always thoroughly searched by the Germans on our return. If you are seen, I will say we brought you back to turn you in, otherwise I will be for the chop, you understand?"

"But I must get back to England," Martin insisted. "I have to get back to the war and, besides, I have two lovely ladies waiting for me."

The wry smile of the captain said everything.

"Here we have a Polish Romeo, Pieter," he said to his second hand. "I'm not sure if we should take him back to our homes. He may steal our wives and sweethearts. Haw! Haw!"

Then he turned back to Martin, serious now: "There is no way we can get you back. If we even dare to go out of our fishing waters, we will be pounced on. We must keep close to shore at all times otherwise..." He gesticulated a knife slitting his throat.

"Jump onto the hold, my friend," Pieter ordered. "You'll be good company for the fish, eh?"

"I'm to go in there with all those fish?" Martin blurted uncomfortably.

"Well, it's either you'll be smelling of fish or dead bodies if the Germans see you," the captain yelled. "Here you are."

He handed Martin some sacking to wrap around him and a length of flexible tubing. "This is so you can breathe under the fish, Romeo Bolenski. They should shatter your thoughts of those lovely ladies. Just lay back and think of England. Haw! Haw!"

The captain was right. When they reached port, the German soldiers were thorough but, as the captain knew, they were not fond of the smell of fish. They gave the holds a couple of prods with a pole and gave the captain the okay.

An hour later Martin was in a hot bath in Pieter's cottage, soon to enjoy a bowl of hot wild rabbit stew. He learned that Pieter lived alone.

He was told, he would have to hide in the cottage until the end of the war, but Martin was adamant he must get back to England.

Pieter had some Germans uniforms in the basement.

"Dragged them up with our nets," he said. "We dumped the bodies back into the drink, but the uniforms can sometimes be useful, you comprehend?"

"I comprehend perfectly, Pieter, and if you have a German pilot's uniform, so much the better."

He thanked his lucky stars, he had learnt how to speak German.

"This is my plan, Pieter." Martin said handing over some scribbled notes, "You like it?"

"What is this? You are mad, Bolenski. You are going to take a German plane and fly to England?"

"S'right, Pieter. The German fighter base is just down the road, right? I have a German uniform and a German accent. Easy!"

Next day, Pieter dropped him near the airfield.

He was in luck. He managed to get through the barrier without being spotted as a dozen or so German pilots were running to their aircraft. They were going out on a quick call, and Martin was with them. In a matter of seconds he had clambered into the cockpit of the nearest aircraft, prompted by one of the ground crew who had primed the engine ready for takeoff. The Messerschmitt was soon airborne, leaving behind a very cross and confused pilot.

When airborne, Martin immediately swung out of the formation and heard the strong words of the German squadron leader over the radio that did not approve at all. To avoid suspicion, he replied he was in trouble and returning to base. But he set his nose for the English coast. His intention was to fly low to avoid the radar. If he could just reach the coast, he could ditch to avoid the risk of being shot down.

Martin thought he had made it when he saw the white cliffs of Dover below. There was some flak from anti-aircraft guns below, but he managed to avoid a hit. Then it happened. Some cocky pilot came up behind his tail. A bloody Spit, too. Thing is, he couldn't defend himself. He would be shooting at one of his own! Normally, he would have spun into a steep dive, turned to come up behind the enemy and fire. But this wasn't the enemy and he couldn't fire back.

The Spit pilot must have thought it was his lucky day. No retaliation and a sitting duck. Martin felt his nose drop. He had been hit in the starboard wing, and the aircraft was floating downwards like a feather. He opened his canopy and clambered out of his cockpit and jumped. His parachute opened immediately, but he landed in the branches of an oak tree sending one of them cracking down through the roof of a barn. He seemed to be okay, except he was dangling dangerously from another branch. Hoards of cattle were marauding from the barn, and two men were running furiously from a farmhouse nearby. They spotted Martin who cried for help.

"That's not one of ours, Jim," one yelled to the other. "Look at his uniform. He's a Hun. Phone the police"

"Okay, Jack. But we've got to get the poor sod down first. He may be injured. Hun or no Hun, haven't you heard of the Geneva convention?"

With the aid of a ladder the two men managed to rescue Martin who was badly bruised behind.

He tried to convince them he was on their side, that he was a Pole and that is why he spoke broken English. But they wouldn't have any of that. He was held at bay with a very threatening hayfork and locked away in a shed, while one of them went to telephone the police.

Martin decided not to stay for the inquisition. He bombarded himself through the wooden door. He just had to get back to base, so made a run for it. He was hurting like hell, but he made it. He found refuge in a large wooded area and collapsed behind the cover of some thick bushes.

After a while he had to admit to himself he wasn't going anywhere. He was in no fit shape to go far. He came across a solitary house where he thought he might find a friendly face. He stripped off his German flying jacket and knocked at the door.

A young woman in her mid-twenties opened the door gingerly. She was very sympathetic and immediately took him in.

"So your name is Martin, is it? Well, Martin, you have certainly had a rough time. I think you pilots are wonderful. Was it a German who shot you down?"

Martin nodded. If he told her the truth, it would only complicate matters.

She gave him tea and some stew, made of knickknacks she said. With the strict rationing it was mainly vegetables and beef cubes, anyway, but Martin could have eaten anything. The young woman told Martin her man was in the army fighting in France. He asked if she had transport; he had to get back to base.

"No, I haven't at the moment. Sorry. My bother has, though. I can try and contact him by phone, but that may be difficult. You don't have to worry, you know," her eyes looked away for a moment until she continued. "You can stay here until the morning. You look to me as though you could do with a nice hot bath and a good night's rest!"

Martin agreed with her generous concern and she showed him to the bathroom. "The water's hot. I was just about to bathe myself, but you first. I will have mine later."

After bathing, he discovered the woman's name was Mary. She supplied him with a pair of pyjamas and dressing gown, which belonged to her husband.

"Sure, Richard won't mind sharing with an ally!" She smiled. She placed everything on the shelf over the boiler after he had changed.

She seemed happy and excited to have someone to talk to. "It's been a long time since I last saw Richard. Nearly a year. He's alright, though. I've just got a letter. I do miss him. It's very quiet here, but I do some work on the land. Good old Land Army, you know, dig for victory and all that!"

Mary wasn't particularly attractive in Martin's eyes. He thought her nose and mouth were not quite right for the face, but she had a nice way about her. The unruly auburn hair looked as though it could do with a wash.

Almost as though she knew his thoughts, she said the boiler would be hot again now for her bath.

"Make yourself at home, Martin. Any books you would like to read… there on the sideboard, please help yourself."

Martin relaxed in front of a roaring log fire. He was almost asleep when he felt a nudge on his shoulder. It was Mary.

"Here's a nice cup of cocoa to see you through the night," she said quietly. "Hope you like cocoa. Richard does."

In the conversation that followed, Martin found peace. It was as if they weren't strangers. Both caught in the vacuum of war, they talked easily about each other, their likes and dislikes, the future, their fears. What followed seemed perfectly natural. It was something between them and, perhaps, for Mary something that could only happen in a wartime situation.

But the following morning, Martin had to make tracks. Mary loaned him some of her husband's civilian clothes and an old bicycle for his journey.

"Perhaps, we shall meet again one day, Martin Bolenski," she looked sad as they exchanged a short kiss. Martin nodded. He could fall in love all over again with Mary, but he knew she loved her husband. It was her husband who had slept with her, not he. By the same token, his lust was for Molly. That is how it was in wartime. Lovers so long apart, substitutes for memories. But he would drop by some time to return the clothes and the bicycle and enjoy some of her special stew. He hoped Richard would return safe. Mary deserved that.

This was some bicycle. The chain was rusty and the going hard, but it was the easiest way to travel the one hundred miles back to base and avoid the authorities. They were looking for a German pilot and, no matter how much he tried, to convince them otherwise without identification, delays were imminent. All he wanted was to return as soon as possible. Mary had seen him off with packed sandwiches and a flask of stew, and he could always find somewhere snug, a barn or an empty house, somewhere to sleep over.

"Martin Bolenski, we've put you down as a goner!" It was Squadron Leader Greg Taylor who first spotted the man on the bicycle, and soon he was surrounded with his colleagues delighted to see him again.

"Forgotten your Spit, Bolly? We've heard you like a good ride but this, a bicycle, a bit over the top, old boy!"

It had been no mean task, the cycling, he was all in. But he had to report to the Commanding Officer who ordered him to go for a check-up at sick quarters. Then he would get some chow and hit the pillow. He thought of June and Molly, and at this moment he felt he loved them both, but the time for decisions was later.

Much to his disappointment, Martin was grounded for another week recovery time.

"Our pilots have to be absolutely fit," the CO barked. "Come back in another week, old boy. Enjoy the break while you can. From what I understand, Jerry is going to take a lot of beating yet!"

June showed Martin she was glad to see him back. Tears filled her eyes when he barged into her place. But why had she given up her job in the NAAFI canteen? She said, she couldn't cope thinking that he may never return. Six months was a long time. That is why she had given up hope, and that is why she ...

"What was that, June?" Martin asked, "That's why you what?"

June was slow to reply, her face saddened, the tears were still there.

"Never mind, Bolly. It doesn't matter now. You are back, and that's all that matters."

God, how could he tell her about Molly, and did he have to tell her? At this moment he wanted June. She was tremendous, and she was still his girl. But there was still Molly, and she still mattered. He was between the devil and the deep blue sea. He had seen Molly the next day. He knew, she had been asking after him, and there were some cryptic remarks from Sgt. Hobbs in the personnel department.

"She knows you're back, so does Molly, Bolly - the elusive girl who craves your charms, no doubt keeping our June on the hook, eh? No wonder she's taken to another!"

"No way, Hobsy," Martin quipped. "I've seen June today. No slandering please!"

"Look, Bolly, I thought you knew. I didn't mean to put the spoke in. Guess it's hard for the girl to tell you. We all thought you were a goner. But it's alright; you've still got Molly by all accounts."

Martin's pride had been shattered. He didn't like Hobbs' attitude, the way he laughed, it wasn't a friendly one. "But she's engaged to me, Hobsy. You sure you haven't got it all wrong?"

"Well, she doesn't wear your ring anymore. Hadn't you noticed?"

Martin had to know. Later he jumped into his MG and was on June's doorstep. But another car was parked in her drive outside the cottage. He recognized it, had seen it around somewhere, but where?

He still had June's door key. June and a bloke were wrapped up on the settee. The disturbed couple looked up. Now he knew where he had seen the car outside. It was Hobbs' car! He turned and stormed out of the room.

He heard June's cries. "I'm sorry, Bolly, but I really thought you were not coming back."

He didn't hear Hobbs telling her it was all right, because Bolly had got another.

Back at his place Martin couldn't fathom how June could have greeted him the way she did on his return. She showed no sign of failing affection for him. How could she be with another chap just hours after they had been together? He decided to be philosophical; he had himself been in two minds, now he knew Molly was the girl for him.

He found her the following day. She never expected to see him again after so long. Didn't even know that he had been reported missing. But her face lit up when she saw him.

"Dad's been ill," she said quietly. "I think the bombing was too much for him. He died a couple of weeks ago with heart failure. First mum, then dad. Times have been rough."

She was crying in his arms. He pulled her chin up and kissed her gently. This was the girl he had been waiting for. This was the girl he really loved.

They shared just two happy years together. The war eventually caught up with Martin. Life expectancy of an RAF pilot was still at a percentage; only the lucky few would survive.

Molly and David stood over his grave. David was eighteen now, had the looks of his father. He expected the tears from his mother and comforted her with a steady arm around her shoulder. Now he was a pilot, following Dads footsteps.

Molly was so proud. At least she still had part of Martin, so her tears turned to smiles.

"That's the spirit, mum. Dad will be happy now," David calmed.

Those Magnificent Gals in Their Bathing Machines

It is simply remarkable, looking back to Victorian time, when they were so coy about showing their bodies in public, how much attitudes have changed.

Maybe not quite so for my generation, having been brought up with the overspill of Victorian discipline, but I do wonder, if those magnificent Victorian gals in their bathing machines could see a present beach scene on a hot summer's day, just how they would react.

Young Millicent Millard was only sixteen when, in June 1850, she was employed as housemaid by a well-known Victorian solicitors family. It was common then for youngsters and sometimes the not so young to be employed as servants to a large well to do family, many of whom were well treated provided they behaved themselves according to house rules and discipline which must be adhered to at all times.

But Millicent, a shy but willing girl, was soon liked by the family and fellow servants. She, in turn, was happy to have found employment in a time when both her parents were unemployed and there were no standard social benefits to fall on, only the few charity organisations usually run by churches of most denominations who, because of the high numbers of those on the breadline, were hard driven to help everybody who begged for assistance.

Her enumeration was meagre like that of the other servants. Even the butler, who maintained top position, was not paid all that much, but it was generally accepted that, because they enjoyed full board and substantial meals and clothing by way of the custom overalls and the like, the staff were well cared for and, indeed, many knew nothing else and were quite happy and content with their lot.

One of Millicent's duties was to assist her mistress and daughter, who was the same age as Millicent, when bathing on the beach nearby.

She, for one, was fortunate to work for a family with high morals with the trend going around that many girls were being taken advantage of because of their vulnerable position. She cried when she heard the case of a girl known to her who was seduced by her master and made pregnant by him, who had since committed suicide because of the smothering of her young baby by a ruthless woman who pretended to help young mothers in her predicament. Millicent confessed to the cook that she would rather just leave and take it as it comes. At least she would not have an unwanted pregnancy.

But never the less, scandal did come her way in another way, when she caught a young lad hiding beneath the bathing hut when it was being used on the sands by her mistress.

"I'm playing hide and seek," he explained, and for a moment Millicent almost fell for it until she realised there was no one nearby to be playing the game with. She bravely saw him on his way, saying she would tell a policeman, she thinking he was waiting for a chance to steal something in the hut. But when the mistress returned from her bathing spree and noticed a hole had been drilled into the wooden floor, it all came to light just exactly what the lad was about. Millicent confessed that she had put a young lad to heel and apologised she had not seen him earlier.

Apologies accepted, she was advised to be more careful in future.

Ironically, the lad would have only got a glimpse of an ankle as Victorian females, especially those of distinction, were very particular about showing any bare flesh whatsoever.

It was considered to be disgusting and very unladylike even to show an ankle, assuming even that could be seen, because apart from bathers being amply covered with the then latest in swimwear, they made jolly sure the wheels of their bathing huts were placed into the water, hiding the view from behind, so that, given the assistance of a servant such as Millicent, they could conveniently slip into the sea.

And if, as often occurred, a scoundrel armed with binoculars viewed the scene from the advantage of the pier to gain a glimpse of the bathers, they would be shielded by their servants. The more high up on the social ladder the more servants, known as dippers, they would show off. But for Millicent it was simply a case of holding out a large towel in which her mistress and her daughter, on coming out of the water, would quickly fold around them.

Some believed the seawater was beneficial to the skin and was also excellent as a tonic.

Later, Millicent described her day as a 'dipper' to Irene, the cook, who was looking at a report in the local newspaper.

"Look at this," she gasped reading aloud. "Two depraved men were today brought to rightful justice for their disgraceful behaviour, seen by PC Bowcroft to be scanning the area of the ladies bathing huts and furthermore. Incredibly, one was found to be hiding beneath a bathing hut."

Then Millicent told the cook how she had to shoo off a fellow hiding beneath madam's hut.

"They must know, men are not permitted within fifty yards of the ladies bathing area."

"Most of them can't read the signs, their excuse!" laughed the cook. "Heaven knows how they could have derived any pleasure from that but that's the masculine animal I suppose."

Millicent said, she learned there was an all-men's beach, too, where they could not 'offend' the female fraternity.

"And even some of them used bathing huts, would you believe," she added.

"Not necessarily for the purpose of changing, either, young Millicent!"

"What do you mean, cook?"

"Not for your young ears to hear," she returned.

By the time a year had passed, Millicent had learned to read with the help and encouragement of her employers. She was keen to discover how bathing huts, also known as bathing machines, came about. She had a keen mind and was fascinated by those who had the ability to invent something that would be a real viable enterprise such as the bathing machine, which was a real money-spinner. Some rented and others sold with 'much profit,' a real pleasing solution for the well to do, enabling them to bathe in the sea with due respectability.

She read that, in 1789, the bathing machine really took off in a big way; it was something for the gentry to be seen using.

The reason? King George III had one especially custom built, and the place favoured for his bathing activities was Weymouth. To be a royal 'dipper' was really something and a contemporary description describes them thus:

"The bathing-machines make it 'God Save the King' their motto over all their windows; and those bathers that belong to the royal dippers wear it in bandeaus on their bonnets, to go into the sea, and have it again, in large letters, round their waists, to encounter the waves. Flannel dresses, tucked up, and no shoes or stockings, with bandeaus and girdles, have a most singular appearance; and when first I surveyed these loyal nymphs, it was with some difficulty I kept my features in order."

It was perceived that the King bathed in the nude for its health giving and odour-reducing benefits. And he was not one for just the constitutional dip; he loved to swim, too, and gave many of his assistants some anxious times.

Millicent was absolutely fascinated and felt truly honoured to be part of the scene, that she was especially chosen to be a 'dipper' for her mistress

They were exciting times indeed. Considerate of her loyal servants who took great care to ensure their absolute privacy, the mistress ordered that all her staff be given turns to partake in the wonderfully stimulating and health giving benefits of the sea. She also ensured the male fraternity were given the opportunity to enjoy the benefits of the bathing machine. The butler and the footman were given special provision to use the machine at dusk, when all was quiet.

So for Millicent, unlike many other contemporaries who suffered abuse and the most horrific treatment, her early years as a lady's housemaid led to that of her being promoted to head maid, which led to her great romance when she was considered cultured enough to become the wife of her master and mistress's son Jeremy, a very rare occurrence indeed in a time when servants and housemaids beneath stairs were kept in their place in a position always subordinate to their employers.

But as times passed and Victorian persuasion dimmed, mixed bathing was the norm and gradually the bathing machines were scrapped or became beach huts.

Come the fifties and seventies, inhibitions dissolved, and swimwear like bikinis, daring beyond the imagination, entered the fashion houses when models lined the catwalk to entice a host of new swimmers.

In the 1950's, when the US did some nuclear weapons testing on islands in the South Pacific, one test that received a great deal of publicity took place on Bikini atoll in 1954. This gave a French designer the notion to call it his new two-piece bathing suit a "Bikini" to cash in on the publicity. Since then, all two-pieces have been called bikinis.

Millicent passed on at the age of fifty-eight but not before she wrote about all her experiences in Victorian England read and cherished with great fervour by her two grandchildren.

Space Relics

The old Ford couldn't have gone any faster. Pete had the accelerator pedal fully depressed, and fifty-five mph was the poor old girl's limit. Well, she had been around forty years or so, like Pete and his co-driver Fritz who shook all over like jelly.

Would they ever make it in time for the one p.m. judging of the classic motor vehicle event in Fenley? Forty miles to go, and it was already twelve noon.

"We shall make it, Pete, with time to spare," assured Fritz.

Tracking a mile behind was old Ginger. He was astride a circa 1935 B.S.A. motor bike with a zeppelin sidecar attached, in which he carried his dog called Amok. Amok was a Cocker Spaniel. He didn't know why he called him that, but it seemed a good idea at the time. Poor old Amok was getting on in years, well for a dog anyway, he was fourteen. His master had just attained the age of seventy. He revved up the engine, and they accelerated with a puff of black smoke, and if he didn't watch out, he would be done by a keen traffic cop for polluting the atmosphere. The noise from the exhaust was like a sudden roar of thunder. He had never ever missed the auto relic's competition yet. Amok barked contentedly. This meant a run into the forest and chasing rabbits on the return trip. He had never caught one, but the spirit was there.

A spacecraft happened to be flying over the area at the time and decreased its speed when the navigator sighted the old ford car and motorbike.

Blamer, the captain, turned to his navigator.

"Look, you must have got the timing wrong again, Clinker. Those vehicles are definitely 1930's to 40's here on the earth calendar."

"No, no, Captain. Look, my dials positively show the year is 2008."

"Hmm. Curious indeed, Clinker. Beam them up, and we'll investigate."

Below, Fritz noticed something. "I don't like to say anything, Pete, but does this thing fly?"

"She used to once but now she only cruises at fifty-five mph. And don't call her a thing. She is a… well, a she, my old lady!"

"No, Pete, I mean fly as in airplanes fly."

"Are you stupid or something, Fritz?"

"Well, I just happened to mention it, because we are flying. Look, we are now at an altitude of approximately ten feet!"

"By George, you're right, Fritz," gasped Pete looking down. "There's life in the old girl yet!"

Ginger was flying, too. Amok barked fearlessly. Ginger looked around. Amok looked first into his master's eyes, then looked downward, ears propped up.

"Gosh, Amok, we're flying!"

"Woof - woof!" agreed Amok, ears fully stretched outwards now.

"Just as we were about to overtake that run-down Ford Poplar," griped Ginger, "which just happens to be flying to show off!"

He burst into song. "Oh! You'll never go to heaven in an old Ford car, 'cos an old Ford car won't go that far."

Amok looked slowly sideways at his master.

"Well, they did it on the old Hollywood musicals, you know," advised Ginger. "One minute there they are just doing your everyday things, the next, they spontaneously started to sing and dance. And don't look now, Amok, but we are flying through the clouds!"

Meanwhile out in front... "You know there's a B.S.A. following, Pete?"

"Birmingham Small Arms, eh?"

"Show off you are, Pete. But I do believe there is a U.F.O. above."

"Don't be daft, Fritz. No such thing." He looked up and saw they were being sucked into a large opening beneath a cone shaped craft hovering above. "Ooher!"

They heard a gushing sound as a large platform, on which they came to rest, closed beneath them. The BSA was there, too, and Ginger and Amok. There were bright flickering lights everywhere and tall thin people watching their arrival. One of them stepped forward and opened the Ford's passenger door and beckoned the intrepid pair inside to step out. Another beckoned Ginger and Amok to alight from the BSA. The two tall men greeted their company with a strong shake of the hand and, in Amok's case, a shake of the paw. He waggled his tail with some gusto, so Ginger was content these folk were alright.

"Don't be alarmed," yelled Ginger to Pete and Fritz. "These folk are okay, look at Amok and how his tail wags. Dogs know these things, you know."

Pete was a trifle wary though. The thin people stood about seven feet tall, their legs and arms were long and wiry, but otherwise the space people were very much like humans except for the eyes. They had wondrous eyes, large blue bowl shaped eyes, which gave out a strong feeling of warmth and kindness. They were very courteous.

"Follow me, please," asked one ever so nicely, and they did.

They were shown into a large mushroom shaped compartment with a central support and were introduced to their Captain and Navigator, Blamer and Clinker, respectively.

"Hello," smiled Ginger. "You are flying saucer people?"

Blamer turned to his navigator with a puzzled expression, and then roared with laughter.

"Of course, that's what you call us, huh? We have it in our data file. We welcome you aboard our craft, Abey 1. Actually, we call them Abeys because they get us from A to B faster than the speed of light."

"Not a lot of people know that," said Fritz in his best Michael Caine accent.

"Glad you speak our language," smiled Pete. "That makes life a bit easier, and it's not every day we bump into a flying saucer... I mean, Abey."

"Sorry to say you're wrong about the language being yours," advised Clinker. "Actually it's ours. Earthlings were derived from our own species. Many years ago, when our planet became overloaded, volunteers were mustered to emigrate to earth, and they took the language with them. All your earthly language variations originated from Viabedes, our home planet. Not that it would matter one eota if we did speak another language."

He pointed to something that looked very much like a computer laptop.

"This computerized brain scan facility is capable of teaching us any language available at the flick of a swatch."

"Really impressive, but it's iota and switch," advised Ginger.

Clinker turned to his captain again, then realised what Ginger meant.

"Well, these slight variations are inclined to happen given a few light years or so, Ginger, but thanks for your keen observation. We will make the appropriate amundments."

"Amendments," advised Pete. "That should be amendments."

The navigator laughed and raised his arms. "We have a number of amendments, I can see. It's been a long time since we used the language, and, no doubt, meanings and spellings have altered."

"You can say that again, Clinker. Have you heard of text talk? It's a whole new concept on the way we communicate, 'especially the youngers," Pete added.

"I can see, we have a lot of catching up to do and updating, Pete."

"By the way, why are we here, Clinker? I mean, have you kidnapped us or something?"

"Sorry, Pete," Clinker replied. "Of course, you will all want to know why we had the audacity to intrude into your earthly lives, and I do hope you will accept our humble apologies. We simply want to settle and argument. Those peculiar vehicles you have with you. They are vintage 1940's? Your earth time, of course."

Ginger told Clinker that wasn't quite right. His was made in 1935, and Pete proudly announced the Ford Poplar he owned was made in 1951.

"But this is 2008 earth time, is it not?" queried Blamer.

Both Pete and Ginger said yes together.

"Is your computer dropping clangers again?" enquired Ginger.

"But why do you drive such old machines in 2008 when you have better models now? The humans have progressed in great strides in a hundred years. It took us much longer."

"But you have space craft technology, Captain, "Pete interrupted, "as yet not invented on earth. We cannot travel the galaxy like you must be able to, because you are here."

"But it took us five hundred years to expand our technology from the first petrol engine to where we are now, Pete."

"I see what you mean. I guess, we are clever clogs then. But to answer your former question, we are partaking in a vintage vehicle rally in Fenley, and, thanks to you, we probably won't make it now."

"Ah!"

Blamer turned to his navigator and was relieved to discover a simple explanation.

"We had noted your new roads on our first scan," he said. "But our second revealed you on a little back road, which gave the illusion we had skipped back in your time."

"Well, our vehicles weren't exactly made for motorways," put in Ginger, "but they have stood the test of time."

"They are indeed time machines, "said Blamer.

"Well, that's a point," Ginger continued. "I would never have thought of them like that. I guess, we could muster up a few vintage relics, Ginger, but this sort of sentimentality does not attract our people."

"Thank you very much for your time. We have done with you now. By the way, don't worry about not arriving at your destination on time. We will put you down on the outskirts of the town you call Fenley, so you will arrive in plenty of time. Thank you all, Pete, Fritz, Ginger, and not forgetting Amok. We have a crewman called Amok, by the way. Please board your machines, and we will see you off. It's been nice meeting you, perhaps another time? Tell you what, we are often in the area. Here, take one of our bleepers, and you will know when we are around. Just be prudent though, okay? You just join us for lunch next time. Just give us a bleep, and we'll pick you up."

It took just one minute for Abey to deposit the vehicles with their occupants in a Fenley field.

They all waved as the spacecraft silently spun upwards.

"What nice people," commented Pete.

"Smashing," agreed Ginger. "Only trouble is, they've dropped us in the middle of this huge field. Where the devil is the bloomin' road?"

"I can see it," yelled Fritz. "Look, there are jeeps and armoured vehicles passing. Must be something to do with the rally, me thinks."

"Strange," put in Pete. "I didn't think they were doing anything on a military theme this year."

"What's that up there, coming down at us," yelled Ginger.

"Crikes," returned Fritz. "Unless I'm mistaken that's a Messerschmitt Bf 109 fighter, circa 1942."

Fritz knew his vintage aircraft nearly as much as his beloved automobiles. The aircraft zoomed so low over them, they could see the pilot inside his cockpit.

"What the hell's going on?" screamed Ginger. "Oh! Blimey, don't look now, but there are a couple of soldiers with raised bayonets coming straight for us. Better put your hands up. Looks like we've been dropped in the middle of a military manoeuvre area. Bloody realistic, though!"

"What the hell do you think you're doing?" an extremely cross red-faced sergeant fanatically yelled. He ordered the wordless trio plus dog to escort him and his corporal to his unit base for interrogation.

They felt like prisoners.

"Don't you think, this is going a bit over the top, mate?" suggested Fritz to the sergeant. "It is just pretend, after all."

"Pretend, pretend? Tell you what, "gasped the sergeant. "I'll pretend, I never heard that. What's your name?"

"Fritz, what's yours?"

"Ah, Fritz, and you speak with a broken German accent?"

"Well, my mother was German. Dad met her after the war during the time he was serving in the British zone in West Germany as it was then, but I didn't realise I had a German accent of any sort."

"The sergeant is just putting you on, he has to be," laughed Pete.

"Quiet!" yelled the Sergeant very dominantly. "This is a serious matter. Now, Fritz, out with it, you are a German spy. You say, your mother and father met in Germany after World War One?"

"World War Two. I'm not that old. Anyway, what's the matter with my mother being German? The Royal Family comes from German heritage, you know. Windsor isn't their real name. They changed it because …"

"Silence, that's sacrilege. This is World War Two. The last was one, so don't try to evade the question, Fritz."

Ginger looked at Pete. Pete looked at Fritz, and Amok looked at them after he had growled at the sergeant.

Ginger was first to speak after a short bewildering and confused silence.

"It must be Captain Blamer's computer still on the blink. The silly so and so's having put us down in the wrong year. What is the year, sergeant?"

"It is 1942, of course. Enough of this! We're holding you until the military police arrive."

"But I wasn't born in 1942 and neither was Pete," appealed Fritz but to no avail, the sergeant didn't want to know.

"What was I doing in 1942?" muttered Ginger, scratching his forehead thoughtfully. "I was just sixteen."

"Enough of the nonsense," interrupted the sergeant. "You're not fooling anyone."

Ginger glanced at Pete and Fritz with a worried expression. He brought his bleeper out of his pocket, the one Blamer had handed him.

"Probably too late, but I'll give it a try. Abey 1 may still be in the area," he ventured.

He never had a chance. The sergeant's eyes nearly popped when he saw the bleeper, and in a second he had grabbed it from Ginger. He closely examined the strange implement.

"What have we here then, Fritz? A new contraption to pass messages to your superiors? Let's see what happens when I press this button."

"He's pressing the contact button," whispered Ginger into Fritz's ear.

"That's alright, Ginger. Abey 1 can sort out the mess they've got us into, assuming they are still in the area, and I can tell them. Watch this!"

With an astonishing movement, Fritz snatched the bleeper from the angry sergeant.

"Blamer. It's Fritz speaking. Beam us up or whatever you do. This in an SOS!"

"Oh! No you don't!" The sergeant snatched back the bleeper and ordered his corporal to place them all under close arrest in the guardroom.

"It's MI5 for you lot, the special boys will want to talk with you. If I'm not mistaken you are all German spies."

As they were escorted away, Fritz noted there was no response from the bleeper, just a hissing noise. Abey 1 must have zoomed out of the area, he assumed. He hoped the craft would soon return, but without the bleeper none of them would know.

They were put into a miserable dark and dank cell pending a visit from what their escort said was the powers that be.

"How can we get through to these guys that we are patriots, even if we could never expect them to accept the truth, that we were from the future?" questioned Pete.

"Search me," Fritz replied negatively. He turned to Ginger again.

"Any ideas mate?"

Ginger nodded. For once he was stuck for words. Amok immediately sensed their predicament. He made high-pitched dog noises. Ginger's right hand came down to comfort him, pulling the animal in close to him.

They all knew their only real hope of escape was to retrieve the bleeper and keep trying to contact Abey 1. Otherwise they would be treated like spies, and anything could happen.

Later, a corporal brought them in a cup of tea, cheese, and biscuits. He hardly said a word, except he knew they were spies and deserved all they would get.

When the corporal left, Ginger noticed that Amok had disappeared.

"The cheeky mongrel. I didn't see him go. Well, I guess that's fair enough. It's impossible for a dog to be a spy surely, and they'd hardly miss him."

"But won't you miss him, Ginger?" Pete asked.

"He knows where we live. He disappeared once before, was away for three days, then he turned up tail between his legs. He knows where his bread and butter is."

"But, Ginger," Pete continued. "Remember this is 1942. Where is home?"

"Of course! That is so stupid of me. He'll be back, just you wait and see. I know he will," Ginger said trying to be brave. But he had a trickle of a tear slide down his cheek.

Later, the three prisoners took refuge under the cover of a blanket in three wooden bunks covered with straw mattresses as a storm brewed outside. Ginger thought about Amok, how he was coping out there in a war stricken land. He remembered stories of how, in France, food rations were so sparse the population took to killing and eating cats and dogs just to survive, but he hadn't heard anything about this happening in Britain. Soon the three were sound asleep.

It was about two p.m. when Ginger awoke with a jump. There was a terrible noise going on outside. Pete and Fritz were also awake.

"What the bloody hell is that? Some storm!"

"No storm, Fritz," Ginger yelled. "There's a bloody air-raid going on. Hear the droning engines and the whistles? They are German bombers bombing the base by the sounds of it. Hope, Amok is alright."

"So this is what it's like in war time Britain," yelled Pete. "Glad I never lived through it."

"But you are now!" screamed Fritz. "Don't worry, we won't be killed."

"You are sure of that, are you?" Pete replied.

"Think about it. How could we be killed in 1942, if at that time we never existed? And Ginger here? If he was killed in 1942, he wouldn't be here now, would he! That is in 2008."

"He's got a point," submitted Ginger.

"I'm not convinced, though," said Pete as the building shook violently and another bomb exploded quite near.

"What's happening now?" yelled Ginger.

"You don't have to shout. You see, it's gone quiet now, the bombers have passed over," observed Pete.

"Exactly," interrupted Fritz. "Too quiet. What's happened to the planes, the barrage? You can hear a pin drop."

"Anyone got a pin?" Pete tried to be light-hearted, but, clearly, he was scared out of his wits.

Then an overwhelming flood of light beamed through the barred windows. But still no noise.

"What sort of lightning is that, with no thunder?" enquired Pete.

Fritz was looking out of the window. "That's not lightning. It's Abey 1! Looks like it's landing on the airfield."

They all cheered heartily. Somehow, Captain Blamer must have realised their predicament, and now they would surely be rescued.

"I don't think so," Fritz said. "I can see the occupants of Abey 1 being escorted by guards and headed this way!"

After a few minutes, Blamer, Clinker, and two colleagues were placed into their cell. The sergeant was very pleased with himself, saying, he had discovered Hitler's latest secret weapon, a strange aircraft indeed. Fritz foolishly welcomed the aliens, and the sergeant suggested they were all part of Hitler's set up to invade Britain, that Mr. Churchill will be very pleased with him indeed to have wrecked the plan. When the sergeant had gone, Pete asked Blamer what the hell they were doing and what about the rest of Abey 1's crew?

Blamer explained the rest of the crew had been dropped off to the mother ship.

Checking the computer, they had discovered a malfunction and realised they had dropped them in the wrong time zone, so they returned to pick them up and return them to their time. They wanted to pinpoint exactly where the three were by honing into their bleeper location. On the bleeper, however, they heard dog noises and discovered Amok on landing with it on his mouth. And then they saw and heard the strange bombing craft with crosses on their wings.

"Who are they, and why do they drop such dangerous explosives that could kill people?" Blamer enquired looking very concerned.

Fritz went into great detail explaining what human war was all about. This war that was caused by a chap called Hitler.

"Well, it's thanks to Amok we found you."

"Suppose that's why Amok disappeared," gasped Ginger. "He was trying to get the bleeper back to us. Where is he now, by the way?"

"No idea," Clinker replied. "Undoubtedly he is a very intelligent animal, and he will return."

"Well, thanks for trying to rescue us, but a fine mess you made of it, if you don't mind me saying!" Fritz squirmed. "Now you, too, have gone and got yourselves arrested."

"We were naïve enough to think they were friendly, that they realised we had prevented those German bombers causing further destruction. This is our thanks."

"How did you do that? Did you destroy the German bombers, Blamer?"

"Destroy? Only you humans can think that way. Our ways are peaceful and none destructive, especially to our own kind, and always have been. It baffles us how anyone would want to kill or maim their own kind. We simply cannot understand the stories written by your writers about 'flying saucers' and the like, carrying aliens from other worlds causing pain and havoc. This would be against the grain. We have discovered, the only real way forward for an intelligent species is by way of peace and cooperation with others. We simply chose to freeze the Germans in their machines. They are suspended in time until we have a chance to see this Hitler, to show him war and destruction bears no fruit in the end. He will surely perish."

"That's a laugh," Ginger said sceptically. "No way will you convince that man. But you were right about him perishing in the end. I've a feeling you will have to go back to the beginnings of man to sort that one out. Man has been destroying man since the year dot and still continues to do so even in our time. But there are many who think like you. Some years ago we had a man called Mahatma Ghandi who had like mind. Peace has to be a solution, but complete and everlasting peace, if only we could learn! Perhaps, time is the best healer."

"If you don't mind me saying, Captain Blamer. I think, Ginger is right. We should let time do the healing."

"I guess you're right, Clinker. But there's no harm in us rendering those machines harmless, that when we defreeze, their bombs will be demobilised. We will make a few amundments to our plan of action."

"Amendments," Fritz corrected.

Blamer laughed. "I will get it right eventually."

"So isn't it about time we got out of here and returned to our time?" asked Pete.

"First we must work out how we get out of this cell," advised Clinker.

"You mean you lot, with all your wondrous technology, can't get us out of here? I can't believe that, surely you have something on you, a stun gun or something like that?" Pete was flabbergasted.

"Nothing. We never believed we would need anything. All we have is ourselves like you, and we are very vulnerable without our technology. But the Mother ship will return when we do not report in and rescue all of us, so please do not be concerned."

"And when will that be?" Pete asked.

"A few days," continued Clinker.

"A few days! Why, we could be dead by then. There must be another way," Pete declared. They all sat and tried to think of something but they couldn't.

"Where's the bleeper? Can't you contact your mother ship with that, Blamer?" enquired Fritz.

"Well, no. Amok must still have the bleeper. Find Amok and we have the answer," Clinker returned.

Where on earth was Amok, and where could he be? An hour passed and another. In the meantime they learned much about Blamer's people, and there was much to tell them about humans.

Pete wanted to stretch. He jumped up, said he had got pins and needles. He held onto the cell vertical bar and stretched upwards. Something rolled from his jacket, a coin.

"Oh! Well, that's my last one-pound coin. Not as though I could spend it, anyway. They had paper notes in the forties."

"I'll get it for you!" interrupted Clinker. "You never know, you might need this coin."

"It's too far out, and you will never reach that, even with your longer than the average human arms," Pete said.

Clinker went up to the bars, did a sort of rolling stance then simply passed between the bars, picked up the coin and returned to the cell.

The three guys looked astounded.

"Do you realise what you have just done?" Pete yelled.

"We can do that. We can dislocate joints and gain access to narrow caves and the like."

Pete laughed. He couldn't believe why Blamer or Clinker hadn't caught on.

"You've just showed us an escape plan, Clinker. Don't you see that?"

They realised just how foolish they had been.

"Sometimes this is a sub-conscious problem with us," Clinker explained. "It is sometimes difficult to see the obvious. I'm sure you humans must suffer from this syndrome as well!"

"Oh! Stop going on, Clinker. Go rescue the keys, and get us out of here. Then you can return us to where we belong."

Clinker did his bit. Everybody waited for about fifteen minutes, eager to see him. Clinker was able to get the keys. He returned with them rattling in his hand.

"Shush!" whispered Pete. "They will hear you."

"There's nobody around," Clinker advised. "It took me a while to find the right keys."

It was easy to escape. Clinker opened the cell door, and they all made for the exit. It was a dark night, and they were soon inside Abey 1.

"Can't believe it was that easy," Fritz exclaimed. "Fine security set up, not as though I am complaining."

"All we need is Amok now," Ginger said. "He has to be around somewhere."

"We can't go back and look, can we, Ginger. That would be foolish," Fritz said. "I know how you feel about him, but if we don't get a move on we are sitting ducks."

"Don't worry about Amok, Ginger. He will be fine," consoled Clinker.

"How do you know?"

"We know these things, Ginger. Trust me."

They were soon off without a sound.

"Just one thing we must do before we leave the area," said Blamer.

Pete, Fritz, and Ginger looked through the large porthole and couldn't believe what they saw. There, suspended in space, were five German bombers. The captain pressed something on his panel and the aircraft instantly came to life.

"For them, it will be as if nothing happened," the captain said. "They have simply been frozen in time. But the horrible destructive explosives they carried have been made harmless. I've fixed it, so that they are unable to discharge the deadly cargo."

"I wouldn't like to be in their shoes when they return to base. They will have a few questions to answer to their commandant," Fritz laughed.

"You are welcome to use our toilet facility, of course," Clinker advised. "You will need a wash and brush up."

"Brush up," Fritz intervened with a chuckle.

"Pardon?" asked Clinker

"Nothing, Clinker, just thank you very much."

"The pleasure is ours, Fritz. This is the least we can do for getting you all into such a mess. Before we return to your time we will feast and drink. You are our very good friends, and we want to be able to call on you again sometime. Perhaps you can come and spend a vacation on our planet sometime?"

"So long as your computer is overhauled," Pete laughed.

"Don't worry. When we return to the mother ship, our complete system will get a wash and brush up, so to speak, and I expect we shall get a new model, the latest in computer technology, no doubt."

After a lovely feast, the three mortal humans were ready to leave. They went to shake hands with Blamer and the rest of the crew but instead received a nose-to-nose 'nudge.'

"Our way of saying farewell to our very best friends," Clinker laughed, seeing their embarrassment.

They were led to their vehicles, which were neatly placed on the dispatch and landing pad in the base of the space ship

"We will beam you down exactly at the time and date we picked you up," Blamer advised. "And, by the way, hope you win your classic vehicle awards."

"Speaking for myself, I don't really care if I don't," Pete said. "Never thought I would say this after being abducted by space people, but I have really enjoyed it."

Fritz and Ginger agreed. It had been the experience of a lifetime and proof that aliens were not bloodthirsty creatures the media made them out to be. They knew they could never make anyone believe their story. Everyone would think they were cranks.

Blamer laughed when Ginger told him that.

"We know better," he said with a certain grin. "By the way, Ginger, haven't you forgotten something?"

"Well, I was worrying and thinking about Amok. Life just won't seem the same without him."

But Amok suddenly appeared, tail up, trotting up to and greeting his master.

"But for him we may never have located you back in 1942. Do you think, we would leave him back here?" smiled Blamer.

They said their final farewells and soon they were back on the road with their machines. They never won anything, but they had made great new friends and looked forward to their next adventure in Abey 1.

Slugs Rule, Okay?

Philip grew accustomed to Jill's idiosyncrasies. He had met her at a pensioners club, and they became friends. Then she invited him to call at her bungalow once in a while for chat and coffee, and that is really all he expected from this very elegant and proper lady.

All went as expected for a while. They had interesting chats, she telling him about her life, her poor husband, Jerry, who had recently died, how she missed him, and her two grandchildren who lived with her only daughter in Canada. Philip told Jill how he had lost his wife, too, just two years before with a massive coronary. Jill said, Jerry had gone the same way.

Philip also had just one daughter whom he hardly saw, living in Florida, but no grandchildren.

The chats and the platonic company suited Philip. At his age he felt that was all he really wanted. Jill was a great conversationalist, and he liked her. But he didn't want to enter into another close relationship.

But soon he discovered Jill wanted more than just conversation and refreshment.

One morning during coffee, Jill joined Philip on the sofa and enveloped into sobs as she reminisced about Jerry and how she missed him tremendously.

Philip's natural instinct was to gently comfort her, just that. He put an arm around her shoulders, and she immediately responded by closing tightly to him. At the time, this meant nothing to him. In the circumstances, it was the natural thing for her to do. But it didn't stop there.

The following morning he awoke with a start. It was in the early hours, barely five a.m. He felt he had dreamt everything that had happened the day before. At least he had managed to get back home despite Jill's reluctance.

"Stay for the night," she had urged.

But Philip wasn't ready for that. He wasn't ready for anything except a plain friendship with the lady, just that and no strings. He was altogether bewildered and confused. He had made up his mind from the start, and he didn't want all that. Well, that's what he concluded...

Breakfasting on toast and corn flakes, he thought about him and Jill and just what had happened. Even now he couldn't believe it. Was it really like that? Thing was, he actually - if he was perfectly honest with himself - enjoyed it. He recalled her words.

139

"Jerry really liked this. As we get older, he said, we don't want all that action stuff, just gentle persuasion as he called it. I thought, maybe, you would enjoy it, too, Philip?"

He kept hearing her and seeing her in his mind. He knew it was no dream, it did happen and it happened to him, so he must sort himself out. Either he was going to continue seeing her, which would probably result in his moving in with Jill, or forget it right now. He must tell her, and he would better not see her again, not like that, anyway. Okay, he cared about her, about hurting her, that she had been hurt enough already, but that was his mind, best to tell her now, from the onset.

He decided to mull on it. He wouldn't meet with her until the afternoon at the club. He had made up his mind by then.

But it wasn't that easy. His encounter with Jill the day before had turned his mind to thoughts he had come to think were redundant. He had lived and loved a happy life with Sue. She was all that a woman could have been, and no one on earth could replace her. He would be happy with just memories.

"Just look at Jill," he told himself. "She's going on seventy, and she's no chicken that you fancy for a bit of good old slap and tickle, is she? She's nice, yes. She has a very pleasant disposition and, yes, I can still recognise her alluring sexuality in those sparkling, not so old looking eyes. Well, that's how they appeared yesterday when she..."

"Don't be daft, Philip Cartwright," he thought out loud. "You are living in the past. Take it upon yourself to be rid of all that, and just enjoy a quiet, peaceful retirement with no complications. That's what you decided upon, wasn't it?"

But after breakfast Jill telephoned.

"Hello, Philip. How are you?" she asked with an alluring tone in her voice and at once Philip felt he was no longer a lone ranger. Someone was taking a real interest in him again. And it was a woman, too. He was sixty, clumpish and slow moving. Not much hair on top, greying at the sides. In the two years since Sue had passed on, he had become very set in his ideas and his ways. There was no room for another trenchant relationship in his life. He just kept telling himself that was the truth of the matter. Yet, for all that, he found himself instinctively sharing joyful conversations with Jill again. And that perfume she used, it just did things to him, he had almost forgotten about!

"I was sorry you had to leave yesterday," she continued. "It was so nice, so very nice to be with a very kind and appealing man again. I told you how I miss Jerry, emotionally as well as physically, you understand. No doubt, I proved that to you. But I've been thinking, I was too impulsive for you. Well, I thought I would just telephone to tell you not to worry too much about the physical part. Give yourself time, Philip."

"Damn! " she continued with an apology for using the word. "How stupid I was to be so dominating, without thinking of your feelings, dear Philip. I admit, I was selfish and stupid and hope you will forgive me for that?"

Philip didn't know what to say or do. His mind was still in a quandary. He did actually enjoy being with her, yes, even if it was different to the kind of love he shared with Sue. Jill was different, that's all, and she enjoyed different things. There had only been one woman. Sue was his first girlfriend and his last. But to him, she was everything.

"Look, Jill. I will be honest. I like you, of course, I do. But I need time."

"But can we continue seeing each other, though, Philip, as long as I promise not to be a burden upon you?"

"Of course. I would like that, Jill. But please don't expect too much of me."

That was the understanding, which, for a while, seemed acceptable to Jill. They still saw each other, even to the extent of Philip visiting her luxury home.

Jill absolutely adored gardening and was proud to regularly show Philip around her herbaceous border, her beautifully varied rose beds, and her large vegetable patch.

"Mind you," she advised, "I knew absolutely nothing about gardening until I married Jerry. Now I feel I have to keep it up for his sake, since he put so much work into it. The patio, the design, he did everything himself and as for his vegetables, well, he was always winning awards for his Cucumbers and his marrows. We always enjoyed fresh produce from the garden."

She paused, turned to Philip with an enquiring expression on her face.

"Any idea on how to get rid of the proverbial slug?"

He thought awhile, scratched his chin and told her about the slug pub. She responded with a bout of laughter, thinking he was having her on.

"No way," he insisted. "They are in the shops now, sort of plastic containers which you slightly fill with this alcoholic substance, although my cousin tells me beer will do. Put them out at night, it attracts the slugs, and they die merrily, drowned in the liquid."

"Takes too long," she snapped. "The number of slugs I have in my garden. It may be a crueller end for them, but I will stick to the secateurs."

"Secateurs?" queried Philip.

"It really is the only way. Messy job, I know, but I simply cut them in half. Much quicker and more humane than the slow death they suffer with most other remedies, me thinks!"

Philip pictured her in his mind, kneeling on the garden path with all those halves of dead slugs around her. Is this the woman he would really like to know on an intimate basis?

"Trouble is," she complained, "I have this obsession with slugs. Look at what they are doing to the cabbages, and that's not all. Just look at my prize dahlias, if you can recognise them as dahlias that is. When Jerry passed on, I bought books and searched the web gardening pages. Then I made for the garden shed. Everything was there how Jerry had left it, all the potting compost, seeds, fertilisers and garden tools. I had to start from square one.

"Everything went well. I was quite proud of my achievement until this year when the horrible beastly slug embarked on destroying all my hard work.

"I tried everything. I knew of to rid the garden of them, but the next morning they always return in abundance. The secateurs treatment is my latest idea , and I will get the better of them, you see if I don't!"

Philip was lost for words, not for the first time with Jill. He had no feelings one way or the other for gardening, although he enjoyed the beauty of flowers and told her so. But he was useless to offer any further ideas as to how to dispose of slugs.

This was the first time he had encountered an embittered and angry Jill. If he had any thoughts about going into a serious relationship with her, her present outburst was a setback.

Sue was never like that, always the quiet tranquil type she took everything in her stead and that was good for him, because, in his earlier days, he tended to be sensitive and short tempered. Sue recognised that and unwittingly found the solution in being just Sue.

How could he cope with Jill then? She was quite the opposite.

As the weeks went by, however, he was becoming more involved with Jill. Thing is, he knew the attraction was mainly sexual. Despite her age and the limitations, it was all rather enjoyable. But as a personality, if he said what he really thought, they would certainly clash.

He was engrossed by her sexual advances. Like a drug he could not do without the simple pleasures she could give and enjoy of him.

But he had to find a way of getting out of the entanglement, knowing that the physical attraction alone could not make for a really sound long-term relationship. He remembered, at this time of his life he wanted just the peace and the quiet of bachelorhood.

That was easier said, or rather thought about, than done. Jill seemed to take him for granted. He was almost like part of the furniture, except somehow he resisted moving in with her.

When he eventually set his mind to telling her firmly that their relationship must end, and on arrival at her place he almost got the words out, it was usually just those few words from her that set his mind into oblivion.

Then for the next hour, he was content with just the simple pleasures she had shared with him, she expecting as if preferring hardly anything in return, save his company and conversation, they endured a few moments of sheer heaven together. Invariably, she would return to her problems with the slugs and, instantly, Philip was back in the real world.

Their pleasure seemed as natural to her as eating meals or doing her daily chores. This was the reason why he could not end the relationship. Yet, he envisaged, given time, the newness of it all would wear thin. Boredom would surely set in, and then he would make his move. But for now he remained the pleasure of her erotic climes, which were his, too.

She never stopped the chatter, though. Sometimes Philip suggested she stopped, just for a while and she would, just for a while. But, inevitably, she returned to the latest slug episode.

"I absolutely loathe and hate those nasty slimy sticky grotesque things," she said, looking up at him, stopping what she was doing. She started to lose concentration, which was unusual because, a creature of habit he had found her to be, she had always kept to a certain mode.

Things were changing. It was the slugs. Thereafter she succumbed into tears and could not bring herself to partake in anything.

"I had this loathsome dream last night, dear. You really must move in with me at the earliest possible moment. I simply cannot abide being so alone at night. Just me alone and those terrible creatures."

"You are referring to the slugs?" Philip asked speculatively.

"No, I am not referring to the slugs, you dimwit!" She immediately apologised, saying she didn't mean that.

"The spiders," she continued.

"The spiders?"

"Yes. Last night, in my dream, but it seemed so real. I'm sure it was on my pillow. I had this dream of a huge, huge spider crawling up my face. Oh! It was horrible, dear."

"It was just a spider, Jill. You mustn't get so worked up. A spider can't hurt you."

"It can't now, because I killed it. I put it down the drain and poured boiling hot water into the sink. I could see its legs clambering to the edge of the drainage hole, even as I poured the hot water over it, it seemed for a while it was never going to lose its grip, that it would never die, that it would come crawling back at me and seek revenge."

"No worry of that, Jill. The hot water would have seen to that."

"It is just that I remember what my mother used to say. She hated killing anything, spiders, beetles, ants, and even wasps. She used to say, they are all entitled to live on earth, and it is not up to us to murder them. She said, if I killed a spider, for instance, all his friends would seek revenge."

"Shouldn't worry about it," Philip eased. "That is just an old wives tale."

"But it is not just the spider, is it. I have killed so many slugs, I have lost count. But I get so cross with them. They constantly vandalise my beautiful, hearty crop of cabbages. I am at my wits' end now. I am getting up at night. It is the best time to get them. I go down to the garden armed with my bright torch and the secateurs. It's terrible, I know, dear, but it is the only way I know that kills them instantly."

"Ugh!" gasped Philip. If he had doubts about moving in with Jill, he certainly had them now, imagining having to put up with that every night.

"So you see, dear. You must move in this week, before I go absolutely mad. I know, only you will calm me and find a real solution as to how finally kill those slugs."

Now was the time, Philip decided, to use his planned excuse to get out of seeing her that week. Well, it would have been awkward, anyway. His brother Tom was coming down to stay for a few days. He needed time with him. It had been years since they last met.

He told Jill the news, and it was if a bomb had exploded. He had never, never heard her use bad language. Thought she was incapable of it. He soon discovered she wasn't.

Now everything came out. All that loving and all that caring and now, what did she get in return?

It was time for Philip to leave, but that was not easy. She threatened him with everything, even attempting to rape her and the like, that he had been constantly pestering her. She would tell everything to the police if he chose never to see her again. Now he discovered her crazy side, and it was as if he had to stay with her, just for one night at least, he thought, anything to take her mind off those confounded slugs.

But during the night she had a dream. Philip awoke with a start hearing her going on about her proverbial slugs, that they were in the bed now, that she felt one on her thigh.

She grabbed the secateurs from her bedside locker drawer, took her imaginary slug by the head with thumb and forefinger and quickly snipped.

A huge yell came from Philip, then silence.

"I'll teach 'em," yelled Jill still half asleep, half awake, "daring to invade my bed."

She made for the garden, oblivious of Philip's agony.

Just two days later the milkman called the police, because Jill's milk had not been taken in.

A policewoman found her lying near the rockery in a pool of blood, surrounded by lacerated slugs, secateurs still clutched in her hand. She looked closer at the body with horror. A stream blood had dried from a large wound upon her forehead. She was quite dead. The officer surmised she had fallen, probably slipped on a slug or two and cracked her head on a rockery stone as she fell.

Then she discovered poor Philip's body in a pool of blood beside the bed.

It was not the fall but asphyxia that killed Jill. At the post mortem a large slug was pulled from her throat.

'Death by misadventure' was the coroner's verdict.

Learning Curves of Life

Looking back on life and thinking about all the moans and grumbles, heartaches, and the rest of it, I guess it is like reading the newspapers, thinking that the whole world is going crazy because news in the media is mainly bad. So it is easy to become paranoid in thinking things are that bad. It is all part of the learning curve, one could say.

I have come to realise that the learning curve is forever, not something you can be done with when you are seventy or something, maybe blissfully believing you know most things.

My wife believes I have nine lives, having nearly lost one in a plane crash, another falling down a lift shaft and the third while undergoing a major abdominal aortic aneurism repair apparently just in the nick of time. The latter making me realise just how fortunate I was to have been living in this millennium when just fifty years ago such an operation would have been impossible.

But providence had it that I was to survive for another innings, the learning curve not completed, and I regained consciousness after a five-hour operation.

Having experienced a horrendous war in my early years, remembering the sheer hell of the indiscriminate bombing by the German war machine in the early forties, I was brought up to hate the Germans and all they stood for and that very nasty Nazi leader called Adolph Hitler and his tribe.

I guess though, if it was for not having been called up for national service at the age of eighteen, I would have just carried on the hate and went along with the media of the time, brainwashing us to treat Germans like they were from another heartless planet, scorning those servicemen who had met and fallen in love with German girls during their service in the British zone of Germany, when bringing them back home to be ruthlessly scorned by everybody, matched only by the hate directed to those white girls who married US coloured guys stationed in England during the war.

Thankfully, it is almost impossible for the present young generation to realise that is how it was and, having met a German girl myself, thinking about marriage and settling down back home, I knew full well what to expect, but felt that if you loved a girl well enough you would overcome all that was thrown at you.

The most significant learning curve for me therefore began in 1953 when, as an RAF medic, I was posted to the RAF hospital in Rostrup, near Oldenburg in the British Zone of Germany.

I went over there cock, sure with the notion we had won the war, and all those horrible Germans would have to bow down to their victors. Young and with erroneous opinions, I was soon to learn that the German people, the ordinary folk who were inadvertently pulled into war by the Nazis, believing Hitler was right for a great country because of what he had done for them, the way he banished a severe unemployment issue bringing happiness and wealth to the nation

If I had any doubts about why the Germans backed Hitler, they were soon dissolved, because in Hitler they saw a great leader, doing so much good for the 'Fatherland.' Given this notion, they could not see any bad in the Fuehrer. Germany was a great country, and he would see to it that Germany would never be humiliated again after the downfall of the First World War.

My learning curve was well and truly served after my posting to the British Zone of Germany, and I will be eternally grateful for that.

Of course, the German folk were not monsters. They were human, just like us and, seeing just how much they had suffered because of the allied bombing, seeing how Hamburg was levelled, made me realise just how futile war is.

We had also suffered the onslaught of German air raids, but that was the name of war, and there was no going back. The war was over, and there were we, just part of the allied plan, sent there to help restore the country, but like the Brits and the spirit given in wartime bombings, the German spirit was likewise, and one only has to look at them now to realise that.

In the early days, my pal and I felt proud to wear our RAF uniforms when taking a trip to Hamburg, naive enough not to understand how the local people would respond. Looking like we were, rubbing in the hurt of war, we stood there, staring at the ruins. I will always remember the way the civilians looked at us. They didn't have to say anything. It was all there in their body language.

We were best out of there, in our truck and back to base, never again to wear our uniform when off duty and in the public eye. Not as though it made a lot of difference, because many could tell we were Brits, anyway.

But already, it was beginning to dawn on me, those Germans were as human as we, that they really were just like us, that ordinary folk were the same everywhere.

Partaking in my duties in Rostrup hospital I had - what I now know - the privilege of meeting some of those ordinary German folk who, because of the war and the scarcity of reasonably paid jobs, were obliged to work as civilian helpers under the auspices of the RAF.

Wilhelm Hoeft was a simple cleaner, very pleasant and obliging, keeping his own counsel. We became friends after I had decided to take down that mask of hate, wanting to see just how people like Wilhelm had come through the war, how they felt about us being there in their country and what that meant to them.

When Wilhelm invited my pal Raymond Vickers and me to his home, we were expecting him to be living in a humble homestead, but this was another reminder of how war had changed lives everywhere.

He told us he was the finance director of a large firm before the war, his house was once a well-kept luxury property with a large acreage of garden. But then it was run down so much, and we could not believe how it was when he rummaged through old photographs, showing us just how it was before the allied troops commandeered the place and many like it during the war.

He also showed us a trunk full of pre-war German Reichsmark notes, which he had drawn from his bank and stashed away in a secret hiding place for safe keeping, but all in vain because they became worthless when the war ended. The Reichsmark was introduced in 1924 as a permanent replacement for the Papiermark. This was necessary due to the 1920s German inflation, which had reached its peak in 1923.

After the Allies defeated Germany, they introduced German Allied Marks (DEA) to replace the Reichsmark and other Nazi currency. However, over issue of the Allied Marks by the Russians led to inflation. The western Allies introduced the Deutsche Mark (DEM) on June 20, 1948, allowing conversion at one Deutsche Mark equal to ten Reichsmark, though with limits on the rights of conversion. The black market rate was around 1000 Reichsmark to the Deutsche Mark. All previous currencies, including the Reichsmark and Allied Marks, became worthless.

So how did Wilhelm feel about it, that he was now having to survive in taking up a common or garden cleaning job with his victors?

But he was such a gentle guy, despite the trauma and having lost his wife with cancer before the war, he was just glad to be of use, and his philosophical aspirations were indeed an example to us all. It made me realise that it wasn't about our being the victors of war but of appreciating the sheer good that came out of the bad, and I shall always remember Wilhelm for that.

And I shall positively remember, having a scar to remind me, the night I was returning to my quarters in uniform, taking a short cut through a spinney and encountering a wild guy who, knife in hand, was intent to kill me. For heaven's sake! Why? That was the question in my mind and instinctively, given the benefit of my service combat training, I was able to defend myself, snatched the knife from my assailant, and overpowered him, but not without suffering a minor wrist injury.

The learning curve of all that was that Friedrich lost his parents during an RAF bombing raid, and it was the uniform he was attacking rather than the wearer. After I had managed to restrain him, we got to talking, and it took a while to explain to him how we Brits had suffered also from the Luftwaffe bombing, how we had friends and neighbours killed. Poor guy, he was at his wits' end, and I didn't blame him. Yet, after all that, we became friends, and through talking about it, we managed to see eye to eye.

He was no murderer; he just needed to get the hate out of his system, more or less as we did with our hate for them.

One of my more emotional learning curves was when I met Ursula, another German civilian who was working in our station NAAFI (Navy, Army & Air Force Institute) as manageress in the café.

We unwittingly got to chatting on a regular basis. I sort of fell for her, and we went for a few walks together around the local lake known as Zwischenahner Meer. It was an interesting time, because Ursula was my first romance, and we had so very much in common. She introduced me to her mother and father with whom she lived in nearby Bad Zwischenahn. They were farmers who had equally suffered the pangs of war, but I was delighted that, because of my nationality, they did not seem to hold that against me.

I wonder what became of them and Ursula, too, because, you see, I introduced her to my best pal, Ian Smith, and he ended up marrying her!

But looking back, well, that learning curve again, it was my first romance. Ursula was a delight, but it wasn't love. But with her and Ian, well, I could see the spark in their eyes, and then I knew.

Ian's ambition, when he was demobbed, was to be a racing driver. He came from Derby, but I lost contact with him after my posting back to the UK in 1954.

Then there was Elfrieda Alexander, also employed with her mother as a cleaner, but that never came to anything, and we were simply friends.

They were times cherished like the occasion I worked as a medic in the Officers Ward. One of the nursing sisters, who were customarily all commissioned officers in service with Princess Mary's Royal Air Force Nursing Service, was courting one of the patients, a flight lieutenant who had undergone a haemorrhoids operation.

Now, the nurses were not supposed to be fraternizing with patients, least be engaged to them, else she would have had to give up her commission, so the embarrassing situation happening when she was on duty and obliged to relieve the officer of a tube which kept his passage open until healed, created quite a traumatic problem, she simply had to confess to me, trusting I would be prudent, and do the business for her.

All was well, and it was well worth the warm hug I got from the relieved nursing sister.

I often wonder if something I had thrown into the Meer is still there. It was a Gestapo pistol I found in the vicinity, apparently where a Gestapo officer had been killed by British troops.

With all that was going on around me, my strong feelings about the casualties of war, I threw it as far as I could into the water.

The war was necessary in the pursuit of freedom and to be rid of one of the most formidable dictators ever.

Perhaps, it is fitting that Germany, despite all the trauma of war, and having the Russians build a wall dividing their land, is now again one of the most successful European countries

It took two big wars to change the aggression in the Fatherland's relentless aim for supremacy over others, but this nation has since arguably achieved that in peaceful competition.

The Writing of "Queen of Misfortune"

When visiting my cousin in Leicester, England, little did I know that her invitation for my wife Daphne and I to join her for a walk in the Bradgate Country Park would lead the way to the publication of my first novel.

The park had a certain charisma about it, the arrangement of the trees, the flora and fauna, and I immediately felt it was a special place. Walking some, we reached the ruins of an old 16th century house. Noticeably, only a small chapel was intact and I realised then what my cousin was about, knowing my interest in old houses, castles, and ruins.

"This is where poor Lady Jane Grey was brought up, Peter," my cousin informed me.

"Who was she?" I asked, faintly remembering the name.

And when she told me, how Jane was brought up there, the corner tower they named the Lady Jane Tower, how she was Queen for just nine days, and how she had her head cut off when she was only sixteen, I was immediately absorbed in anything to do with her.

What on earth made the bloody Queen Mary Tudor give the instruction to execute Jane and her husband Guildford? I would soon find out, that was sure!

My cousin seemed surprised we had not heard of her but then, living in the vicinity, it was unlikely that she wouldn't have known of her, of how she was duped by the wicked John Dudley, the Duke of Northumberland, to take the crown after the death of the boy King Edward, not seeming to realise he had not the support of the people in his quest to prevent Mary Tudor, King Henry VIII's eldest daughter by his first wife, Catherine of Aragon, to take her rightful claim to the throne.

I decided then, I just had to write something about this wretched girl who had been almost forgotten, and rarely mentioned in the annals of history, she had had a very rough deal here on earth and deserved more recognition for that which she had to endure.

I became obsessed with my subject, researching every avenue open to me both on the Internet and reading other books, which had been written about her. Until that time, I had assumed much of that which has been written of her was reliable and authentic, but it was not going to be that easy by any measure of the imagination.

Putting aside fictitious accounts of Jane's life, how she was brought up, and her marriage and so on, I discovered that which was said to be true often differed with other accounts, and for some time I was utterly confused in my quest to gather as much fact as I could muster of her.

I knew from the start that much of my book would have to be fictional, because her life was so very short and not all that much had been chronicled of her. I needed a skeleton of truth, like the various letters written by her in different forms, a prayer, her speech from the scaffold and letters written by her tutors, and other sources as displayed in the British Museum

And then came the task in trying to make something legible of those sparse facts. Many authors give a romantic account of Jane's association with Guildford Dudley whom she was forced to marry against her will.

I wanted to trace hints of what might have been. For example, there came an uncomplimentary reaction when she was advised she would have to marry Guildford, enough to convince me that she positively did not want the marriage when she declared that she was betrothed to Herbert, the young Earl of Hertford.

Then there were hints of a great admiration of her tutor, John Aylmer, in Roger Ascham's written account when he visited Jane, and she was alone in Bradgate whilst her parents were out hunting. This spurred me to create in my novel a more meaningful relationship which, when she grew to be a woman, accepted then to be at the age of fourteen, became a love match, thus giving me an ideal romantic string in my book.

I read also of a 'stranger' in the crowd when Jane was on the scaffold awaiting her execution, a stranger who climbed up to assist her when blindfolded, when on her knees, she was unable to find the block. It seemed probable that a disguised John Aylmer could have been the stranger, so I have made him so in my book.

I discovered a number of hints that led me to write what I imagined of Jane could have been true.

Returning to Bradgate, I needed to be alone to capture something, which may just bring her alive in my thoughts, to help me give a good and respectful account of her life there. And I was not disappointed. I spent a whole day there just sauntering around and getting the feel of the ruins and the surrounding area. I felt somehow her body had been returned to a special place where she picnicked with her guardian and nurse, Mary Ellen. There is the story of a horse and cart, which appears as an apparition late every New Year's eve. Maybe it was transporting the body of Lady Jane to her burial place?

When I looked around the old boundary walls of Bradgate house, it wasn't long before I felt the need to kneel and pull up some turf there to find the stump of a long felled tree, and then, a little distance apart, I found another and then another until I realised there had been a circle of trees in the area, and I was drawn to the centre where I felt strongly her remains had been interned. But there was a huge clump of spiky bramble preventing me from stepping into the centre. It felt to me that the centre area was sacrosanct and must not be disturbed, which made me all the more convinced her remains were there.

I wrote a letter published by the Leicester Mercury, asking for information regarding Bradgate's connection with Lady Jane Grey. One response from a gentleman, who lives in Leicester, mentions a time he and his wife were walking around the boundary wall there. They heard a young child crying over the other side of the wall. On clambering up the wall and looking over the other side however, he could see nothing. The couple suggested I wrote to the park ranger who, they advised, kept a record of ghostly happenings and sightings. But when I followed this up, the ranger denied this and suggested the sound attributed to a crying child was probably that of a peacock, several of which inhabit the area.

The most unusual and exiting reply came from the friend of an American girl who claimed to be Lady Jane in her former life. Because at the time I was so very involved and absorbed I had a thought of what if? This would be indeed a writer's dream if it could be somehow verified, which in reality was of course unlikely, but nevertheless I gave it a go and wrote to the party concerned and, surprise, surprise - no reply!

I discovered much about the architecture of the house, how it was the first brick building to have been built since Roman times, most of them in that century having been constructed of stone.

A man-made lake had been dug around a natural well to the rear of the house on a slightly higher plain which, given the natural influence of gravity, enabled the supply of running water through a series of clay pipes beneath the floor, which could be pumped up as required, a facility regarded to be a sheer luxury in those days.

On the day I went to Bradgate visitors were sparse, so I was able to spend time just meditating in effort to draw in something, but it is not easy, when you want something to happen, that the mind plays irrational tricks. So I tried to keep level minded, hoping that Lady Jane, if her spirit was still there, would transmit something, anything to me. I moved over to what once was a spiral staircase leading to what was said to be her apartment in Lady Jane's Tower. I stood there motionless, just listening, feeling and hoping, but I felt nothing, but I did rub my fingers along the few bricks and mortar which remained, and there I did feel something, like the mortar had been grilled out and something hidden inside, but, needless to say, there is no evidence of this.

But I have used the idea in my book relating to a message received by Jane of her father, which seems to merge well with the rest of the chapter. So could it be, there was actually something implanted there, was there something very faint itching to get through to me?

I had to conclude, why would Jane want to return to a place where for much of the time she was unhappy and beaten by her parents? But there was a romantic twist in my story of her relationship with John Aylmer. So that was a reason she could come back occasionally, if my theory was true. But it is never that easy and, no matter what, nothing could be confirmed. I just had to get on with it and do my best, with the knowledge that Jane really wanted me to write something about the truth of how she was duped by John Dudley and forced into an unwanted marriage to his son.

To gain some inherent mood, imagining how those last days must have been like for the Lady Jane, I visited the Tower of London so see the house in which she was imprisoned. I really needed to get into the building and enter the upstairs apartment to imagine the true feel of the place, look through the window she would have peered through to see the erection of her scaffold and the return of her husband's decapitated body after he had been executed on Tower Hill. Imagining how she must have felt that day on the 13th February 1554, stepping down those stairs and entering the courtyard so bravely and graciously.

But regretfully, this was not possible, so I had to create the scene as it might have been as I looked at the scaffold scene on the green adjacent to the Chapel Royal of St. Peter ad Vincula where the body of Jane of Royal Blood should have been buried beneath. I believe, Queen Mary Tudor prevented this and her body, left for hours afterwards on the scaffold, was removed by persons unknown and it was returned to Bradgate.

When in Queen Victoria's reign, the floor was raised, they discovered the skeleton of a small woman which were first thought to be of Lady Jane but later found to be those of Ann Boleyn who was also executed there.

Then there was the probability of her portraits, two or three, that were said to have been done and to be of her. But I could find no absolute proof of that, and I have come to the conclusion that Queen Mary Tudor was so unhappy and guilty about having authorised the execution of her cousin Jane, she ordered the destruction of anything she could find relating to her.

The difficulty was in trying to imagine how she would have looked until, eventually, there was a brief mention by a French ambassador attending her coronation, that she was small, standing just over five feet and demure with a pale complexion, red hair, and freckles.

So much of the material was now to hand, and I felt I could master the challenge and start to write something I would call a faction piece because it is fiction very much based on hard researched and gained fact.

Three years later, given the immense patience and understanding of my wife Daphne, I completed the book, and feel I have given of my best a near truth account as possible of this unfortunate nine day Queen.

CPSIA information can be obtained at www.ICGtesting.com
Printed in the USA
LVOW070145281112

309059LV00022B/1754/P